Writing the Critical Essay

School Shootings

An **OPPOSING**VIEWPOINTS® Guide

Lauri S. Friedman, *Book Editor*

OPPOSING VIEWPOINTS® SERIES

GREENHAVEN PRESS
A part of Gale, Cengage Learning

GALE
CENGAGE Learning·

Detroit • New York • San Francisco • New Haven, Conn • Waterville, Maine • London

Christine Nasso, *Publisher*
Elizabeth Des Chenes, *Managing Editor*

© 2010 Greenhaven Press, a part of Gale, Cengage Learning

LIBRARY OF CONGRESS CATALOGING-IN-PUBLICATION DATA

School shootings / Lauri S. Friedman, book editor.
    p. cm. -- (Writing the critical essay, an opposing viewpoints guide)
  Includes bibliographical references and index.
  ISBN 978-0-7377-4564-1 (hardcover)
  1. School shootings--United States--Juvenile literature. 2. Essays--Authorship--Juvenile literature. I. Friedman, Lauri S.
  LB3013.32.S347 2010
  371.7'82--dc22
                                                                        2009028333

Printed in the United States of America
1 2 3 4 5 6 7 13 12 11 10 09

CONTENTS

Examining the state of writing and how it is taught in the United States was the official purpose of the National Commission on Writing in America's Schools and Colleges. The commission, made up of teachers, school administrators, business leaders, and college and university presidents, released its first report in 2003. "Despite the best efforts of many educators," commissioners argued, "writing has not received the full attention it deserves." Among the findings of the commission was that most fourth-grade students spent less than three hours a week writing, that three-quarters of high school seniors never receive a writing assignment in their history or social studies classes, and that more than 50 percent of first-year students in college have problems writing error-free papers. The commission called for a "cultural sea change" that would increase the emphasis on writing for both elementary and secondary schools. These conclusions have made some educators realize that writing must be emphasized in the curriculum. As colleges are demanding an ever-higher level of writing proficiency from incoming students, schools must respond by making students more competent writers. In response to these concerns, the SAT, an influential standardized test used for college admissions, required an essay for the first time in 2005.

Books in the Writing the Critical Essay: An Opposing Viewpoints Guide series use the patented Opposing Viewpoints format to help students learn to organize ideas and arguments and to write essays using common critical writing techniques. Each book in the series focuses on a particular type of essay writing—including expository, persuasive, descriptive, and narrative—that students learn while being taught both the five-paragraph essay as well as longer pieces of writing that have an opinionated focus. These guides include everything necessary to help students research, outline, draft, edit, and ultimately write successful essays across the curriculum, including essays for the SAT.

Using Opposing Viewpoints

This series is inspired by and builds upon Greenhaven Press's acclaimed Opposing Viewpoints series. As in the parent series, each book in the Writing the Critical Essay series focuses on a timely and controversial social issue that provides lots of opportunities for creating thought-provoking essays. The first section of each volume begins with a brief introductory essay that provides context for the opposing viewpoints that follow. These articles are chosen for their accessibility and clearly stated views. The thesis of each article is made explicit in the article's title and is accentuated by its pairing with an opposing or alternative view. These essays are both models of persuasive writing techniques and valuable research material that students can mine to write their own informed essays. Guided reading and discussion questions help lead students to key ideas and writing techniques presented in the selections.

The second section of each book begins with a preface discussing the format of the essays and examining characteristics of the featured essay type. Model five-paragraph and longer essays then demonstrate that essay type. The essays are annotated so that key writing elements and techniques are pointed out to the student. Sequential, step-by-step exercises help students construct and refine thesis statements; organize material into outlines; analyze and try out writing techniques; write transitions, introductions, and conclusions; and incorporate quotations and other researched material. Ultimately, students construct their own compositions using the designated essay type.

The third section of each volume provides additional research material and writing prompts to help the student. Additional facts about the topic of the book serve as a convenient source of supporting material for essays. Other features help students go beyond the book for their research. Like other Greenhaven Press books, each book in the Writing the Critical Essay series includes bibliographic listings of relevant periodical articles, books, Web sites, and organizations to contact.

Writing the Critical Essay: An Opposing Viewpoints Guide will help students master essay techniques that can be used in any discipline.

School Shooters in Their Own Words

More than 320 school shootings have occurred in the United States since 1992, making it easy to understand why Americans are desperately looking for answers to what could make a young person kill innocent students and teachers. Part of what makes it so difficult is the fact that school shooters rarely live to tell their story—many kill themselves before they can be apprehended by police. In some cases, however, school shooters have been arrested alive or leave posthumous messages. Their words reveal clues to what motivated them to kill and whether they regret their actions.

Shooter Seung-Hui Cho fatally shot himself after killing thirty-two people at Virginia Tech, but he left a lot of material behind for police and social analysts to study. On the morning of April 16, 2007, Cho went to West Ambler Johnston Hall, where he shot and killed two people at around 7:15 A.M. Then he returned to his dorm room and assembled a package of photos, videos, and an eighteen-hundred-word document. He took the package to the post office and mailed it to NBC News before continuing on his shooting spree, which to date is the worst school shooting in American history.

The contents of this package offer some insight into what motivated Cho to kill his fellow students and teachers. In addition to being mentally ill and delusional, it is possible that Cho's disdain for the privileged, wealthy students at Virginia Tech possibly played a motivating part in his decision to kill. The videotape features Cho ranting about his hatred for spoiled, rich college kids, indicating that the behavior and status of his schoolmates had somehow driven him to murder them. He also indicates that being ignored by his classmates had somehow forced him to act: "You had a hundred billion

A young man grieves at the memorial of 32 granite blocks representing each of the people killed on the Virginia Tech campus on April 16, 2007.

chances and ways to have avoided today," he said on the tape. "But you decided to spill my blood. You forced me into a corner and gave me only one option. The decision was yours. Now you have blood on your hands that will never wash off."[1]

He also gave some indication that he thought of himself as a great martyr who was dying for a noble cause: "Thanks to you I die, like Jesus Christ,"[2] he said. The photos he sent show him waving a hammer, putting a knife to his neck and gun to his head, and pointing guns at the camera. Cho left behind more information than most school shooters, though it is still insufficient to truly understand what could have led him to kill so many innocent people.

Feeling outcast and hurt by other students was also the reason shooter Elizabeth Bush gave for opening fire in her Pennsylvania high school cafeteria, where one hundred of her fellow students were eating lunch. Bush is rare both for being a female shooter and for not killing herself after the 2001 attack, which wounded just one of her fellow students, her friend Kim Marchese. Bush said she targeted Marchese for telling other students that Bush secretly enjoyed cutting herself. "She was laughing. She was calling me a freak and all this stuff," remembers Bush. "I was very hurt that she'd do that to me . . . those feelings, those thoughts that I told her, they were never supposed to be revealed to anybody; and that's what she did."[3]

Eventually, a classmate who rode the bus with Bush talked her into dropping the gun, even though Bush had fantasized about killing herself in front of Marchese. After serving a three-year sentence in a juvenile facility, Bush felt she had become a productive member of society and deeply regretted her actions: "It plays over, over and over all day and all night," she said. "And it hurts me because I hurt somebody else."[4]

Another shooter who lived to tell his tale is Charles "Andy" Williams, who killed two of his fellow students and wounded thirteen others at a San Diego–area high school on March 5, 2001. Williams had reportedly saved a bullet to use on himself but was apprehended by police officers in the school bathroom before he had the chance. Williams was disturbingly nonchalant about murdering his fellow classmates, as is revealed in the following conversation he had with Detective James Walker just hours after he was arrested:

Walker: "OK, you wanna tell us what all this was about?"
Williams: "Mmm, I was just mad, I guess."
Walker: "Why—why shoot them?"
Williams: "They were just there."
Walker: "Wrong place at the wrong time, huh?"
Williams: "Yeah."[5]

Williams is now serving a fifty-year sentence—he will not be released from prison until the year 2052, when he will be sixty-six years old. Unlike school shooters who included themselves on the victim list, Williams has had the opportunity to reflect on his crime and try to make amends for it. In his first year in prison, he read 159 books and took in-prison classes, maintaining a grade point average of 3.09. He has also expressed an interest in earning a college degree in theology and becoming a pastor in prison. Like Bush, Williams has also come to regret his actions: "It was a stupid thing to do," he said a year after the shootings. "I wish I never did it."[6]

Sadly, Cho, Bush, and Williams are just a few of the young Americans who have perpetrated this ghastly, and growing, crime. What motivates school shooters, as well as what measures can prevent school shootings, are among the topics explored in *Writing the Critical Essay: An Opposing Viewpoints Guide: School Shootings*. Model essays and thought-provoking writing exercises help readers develop their own opinions and write their own cause-and-effect essays on this unfortunate yet timely subject.

An Amish funeral procession of horse-drawn buggies for a victim of the Amish school shootings in 2006 travels thru Georgetown, Pennsylvania, on its way to the cemetery.

Notes

1. Quoted in William M. Welch, "Va. Tech Gunman Sent Material to NBC," *USA Today,* April 18, 2007. www.usa today.com/news/nation/2007-04-18-virginia-tech_N .htm.

2. Quoted in Welch, "Va. Tech Gunman Sent Material to NBC."

3. Quoted in Connie Chung, "Sticks and Stones: School Shooter Explains What Drove Her to the Edge," ABC News.com, March 7, 2001. www.antidepressantsfacts .com/2001-03-07-ABC-BethBush.htm.

4. Quoted in Connie Chung, "Sticks and Stones."

5. Quoted in Greg Moran, "Williams Reluctant to Discuss Past, Future," *San Diego Union Tribune,* August 18, 2002. www.signonsandiego.com/news/metro/santana/ 20020818-9999_1n18andy.html.

6. Quoted Moran, "Williams Reluctant to Discuss Past, Future."

Section One: Opposing Viewpoints on School Shootings

Gun-Free Zones Prevent School Shootings

DeWayne Wickham

In the following essay DeWayne Wickham argues that guns should not be allowed on or near school campuses. He explains how some school administrators and legislators have proposed allowing teachers and students to carry guns on school campuses. In Wickham's opinion, this is dangerous and scary. Schools for the most part are very safe places, but they will become infinitely more dangerous if teachers and students are allowed to carry guns, he warns. Neither teachers nor students are trained to use such weapons, and it is very likely the weapons will be stolen or used to resolve personal conflicts. Wickham argues the best way to keep schools safe is to designate campuses as gun-free zones and to hire professional security officers trained in weapons use and violence prevention to patrol school grounds.

Wickham is a columnist for *USA Today* and the Gannett News Service.

Consider the following questions:

1. What does Wickham say leaders in Harrold, Texas, have proposed that teachers be allowed to do in public schools?
2. What do Superintendent David Thweatt, Representative Joe Driver, and Governor Rick Perry all have in common, as reported by Wickham?
3. What does the word "nonfeasance" mean in the context of the essay?

N o good will come of these bad ideas.

When children return to school in Harrold, Texas, later this month [August 2008], they might find some teachers are hauling more than textbooks into the classroom. Leaders of the tiny North Texas school district have given teachers the go-ahead to carry concealed weapons on campus.

The district, which has about 50 teachers and staffers, won't reveal how many will be bringing guns to school. The superintendent said he wants to keep that a secret from potential attackers—and students.

Superintendent Thweatt's decision to arm teachers was controversial because many believe introducing guns into schools will cause more mass shootings.

Arming Teachers and Students Is Scary

"When the federal government started making schools gun-free zones, that's when all of these shootings started," Superintendent David Thweatt told *The Associated*

Press. "Why would you put it out there that a group of people can't defend themselves? That's like saying 'sic 'em' to a dog."

Thweatt presumably was referring to high-profile school shootings like the one in which a deranged student killed 32 people and himself at Virginia Tech [in 2007], and a 1999 rampage by two students at Columbine High School in Colorado who killed 12 students and a teacher before committing suicide.

In 1990, the Gun-Free School Zones Act made it a federal crime to bring a gun into a school zone. But the Supreme Court ruled the law unconstitutional in 1995, well before the Colorado and Virginia school shootings.

Even while the Harrold school district is putting guns in the hands of public school teachers, an influential Texas state legislator wants to arm college students in the Lone Star state. Back in July, state Rep. Joe Driver, who chairs a committee that considers gun bills, said he thinks it's a good idea to allow college students with concealed gun permits to take their pistols to class.

> ## Fewer Guns Would Mean Fewer Shootings
>
> There are things we can do to make it harder for dangerous people to get guns. Many criminals—even mass killers like the Jonesboro or Virginia Tech killers—still go through legal channels to get firearms every single day. Strong, common sense gun laws could help stop them.
>
> Paul Helmke, "When a School Shooter Seeks a License to Carry a Loaded, Concealed Handgun," HuffingtonPost.com, December 23, 2008. www.huffingtonpost.com/paul-helmke/when-a-school-shooter-see_b_153194.html.

That would deter bad guys, he said, because they wouldn't know who's packing and who isn't. Texas Gov. Rick Perry agrees. He supports the idea of allowing college students and public school teachers to carry guns to class.

I think this is all very scary.

Most Schools Are Safe Without Guns

Putting guns in classrooms from kindergarten to college, I fear, will produce many more violent confrontations than they might prevent. As horrific as the Columbine and Virginia Tech shootings were, they are rare events.

For the vast majority of students, this nation's schools are safe. And schools threatened by violent behavior

Americans Are Pessimistic About School Shootings

A Gallup poll revealed that in the six years that elapsed between the 1999 Columbine and 2005 Red Lake, Minnesota, school shootings, Americans became less hopeful that anything could be done to prevent school shootings and thought it likely that more school shootings would occur in the future.

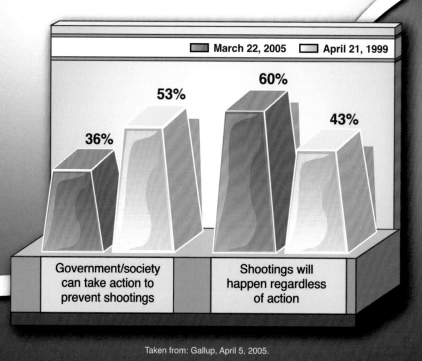

Taken from: Gallup, April 5, 2005.

from students—or by attacks from nonstudents—would be better protected by a trained security force.

School officials and government leaders who want to put guns in the hands of students and teachers shirk their responsibility. Keeping schools safe is their job, and it's their duty to provide adequate security. Instead, they cloak their nonfeasance in muddled talk of a constitutional right to bear arms.

Such talk can produce good political theater. It also obscures the fact that—as in Texas—school officials and state government leaders aren't doing their jobs.

Security Personnel Should Protect Students

If school officials in Harrold want to make schoolchildren more secure, they should give that responsibility to trained personnel instead of pushing it onto gun-toting teachers. Those teachers have enough to do as it is.

Texas governor Rick Perry gives a pro-gun speech at Texas Tech University. Perry's belief that students and teachers should carry guns to class is hotly debated.

TEXAS TECH

And if Perry and Driver see a need to make Texas colleges safer, they ought to use the powers of their office to beef up campus security forces. What they shouldn't do is back a call for something as random, unpredictable and potentially dangerous as allowing students to carry concealed weapons on campus.

Analyze the essay:

1. Wickham characterizes gun-toting teachers and students as "random, unpredictable, and potentially dangerous." What does he mean by this? Do you agree with him?

2. In Wickham's opinion, letting teachers carry guns is likely to result in more school shootings, not less. Do you agree that arming teachers would have this effect on school shootings? Why or why not?

Gun-Free Zones Cause School Shootings

Larry Elder

Gun-free zones attract school shooters, argues Larry Elder in the following essay. He recounts several school shootings in which shooters were stopped only when someone with a gun came on the scene. But because schools are gun-free zones, these people had to run to their cars or other off-campus locations to retrieve their guns. Elder argues the shootings could have been stopped sooner, and lives could have been saved, had these people been allowed to carry their weapons on their persons on school grounds. In addition, Elder cites statistics that show most criminals say they avoid targeting places where people are likely to have guns. In Elder's opinion, forcing schools to remain gun-free makes them an easy target for school shooters.

Elder is an attorney, columnist, and syndicated radio talk-show host. He is also the author of *Showdown: Confronting Bias, Lies, and the Special Interests That Divide America.*

Consider the following questions:

1. Describe what happened at Pearl High School in Mississippi. How does this factor into the author's argument?
2. According to the National Institute of Justice, what percent of felons say they avoid robbing houses if it seems likely they will get shot?
3. What is Israel's policy on weapons in schools?

Larry Elder, "Do 'Gun-Free' Zones Encourage School Shootings?" *Human Events*, October 18, 2007. Copyright © 2007 Human Events Inc. Reproduced by permission.

This time, Cleveland.

A 14-year-old suspended high school student entered Cleveland's Success Tech Academy, a gun in each hand, and opened fire, wounding four. Later, we learn that the shooter's past included violent confrontations, mental problems and at least one previous suspension. A month earlier he told a friend that he intended to shoot up the school. But no one, apparently, took his behavior seriously enough to notify authorities.

Gun-Free Zones Are Easy Targets

Meanwhile, a high school teacher in Oregon, with a permit to carry a concealed weapon plus training, sought permission to carry her firearm to school. In fear of her ex-husband, against whom she filed and received two restraining orders, she wanted the ability to protect herself in the event he showed up. Furthermore, she argued that even without the fear of her ex-husband, the Second Amendment and Oregon state law allow her to carry her firearm to work. Her school district, however, prevents her from carrying a firearm to school.

This raises a question. Do shooters consider schools "gun-free zones"? Do they consider it unlikely that any authority figure—whether teachers or, in some cases, security guards—poses an armed threat? But in some school shooting cases, guns helped to end shooting sprees and minimize loss of life and injury.

Guns Prevent or Stop Shootings in Progress

Edinboro, Pennsylvania. A 14-year-old middle school student opened fire at a school graduation dance, being held at a local restaurant. The shooter killed one teacher and wounded two students and another teacher. The armed teenager was apprehended by the restaurant owner, who grabbed his own shotgun from his office and went after the shooter. Staring into the owner's shotgun, the teen dropped his gun and surrendered.

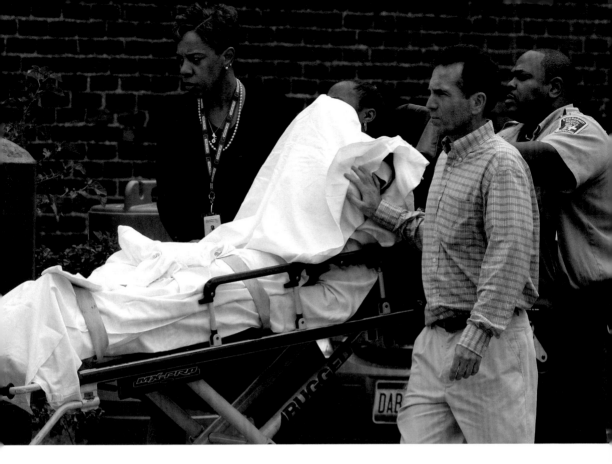

Pearl, Mississippi. A 16-year-old sophomore entered Pearl High with a hunting rifle under his overcoat. He opened fire, killing two students and wounding seven. The assistant principal, Joel Myrick, ran to his truck and retrieved the .45 automatic he kept there. Running back, he spotted the shooter in the parking lot. Ordering the teen to stop, the vice principal put his gun to the shooter's neck and held him until police arrived.

Grundy, Virginia. At Appalachian Law School, a disgruntled student on the verge of his second suspension entered a school building and shot and killed the dean and a professor. He then shot four students, killing one. Hearing the shots fired, two students, Michael Gross and Tracy Bridges, ran to their cars to retrieve their guns. With guns aimed at the shooter, Bridges ordered him to drop his weapon. When the shooter turned and saw Bridges' gun, he laid down his weapon and put his hands in the air.

A victim of the Cleveland Success Tech shootings is wheeled to an ambulance after a fourteen-year-old student entered the school and opened fire, wounding four students.

Criminals Avoid Places Where People Carry Guns

Professor and economist John Lott checked 280 separate news stories in the week after the Appalachian Law School shooting, and only found four that mentioned the students who stopped the shooter had guns. The *Washington Post*, for example, said the students "helped subdue" the killer.

Pearl High School assistant principal Joel Myrick, at podium, relates his experiences in apprehending at gunpoint his school's shooter who killed two and wounded seven.

Newsday wrote the shooter was "restrained by students." The *Richmond* (Va.) *Times-Dispatch*, however, wrote that the shooter "was wrestled to the ground by fellow students, one of whom aimed his own revolver at [the killer]." Four months later, the *Times-Dispatch* detailed the students' actions, including the second student's use of a gun.

What do felons think about an armed citizenry? A survey of convicted felons by the National Institute of Justice found 74 percent of the felons agreed that, "One reason burglars avoid houses when people are home is that they fear being shot during the crime."

The survey also asked these felons whether they had abandoned at least one crime because they feared the intended victim might be armed. Thirty-nine percent said they abandoned at least one crime; 8 percent had abandoned such a crime "many" times; 34 percent admitted being "scared off, shot at, wounded, or captured by an armed victim"; and nearly 70 percent knew a "colleague" who had abandoned a crime, been scared off, been shot at, wounded or captured by a victim packing heat.

A survey of 23,113 police chiefs and sheriffs across the country found that 62 percent of these top cops agreed that "a national concealed handgun permit would reduce rates of violent crime." About 80 percent of rank-and-file police officers, according to polls, support the right of trained citizens to carry concealed weapons.

We Must Let People Shoot Back

No siren or email campaign or lockdown is going to stop a mass murderer. Just like Columbine, not a single police officer was able to engage [Virginia Tech shooter Seung-Hui Cho]. Let's embrace the U.S. Constitution, not ignore it. Let's fight evil with might and force. We have to shoot back.

Mike Gallagher, "Preventing Another Massacre," Townhall.com, April 20, 2007. http://mike gallagher.townhall.com/columnists/MikeGallagher/2007/04/20/preventing_another_massacre.

No Shootings at Armed Schools in Israel

Israel gets it. Since the 1970s, on school campuses in Israel, policy requires teachers and parent aides to arm themselves with semi-automatic weapons. The result? School shootings have plummeted to zero.

As for Cleveland, would allowing authority figures to arm themselves have resulted in reduced casualties, or perhaps even deterred the shooter in the first place? No one can say for sure. But no doubt at least some Cleveland parents now believe the benefits of armed campus adults outweigh the costs.

Analyze the essay:

1. Elder argues that criminals abandon crimes when they fear their victim might be armed. How do you think DeWayne Wickham, author of the previous essay, would respond to this argument?

2. Elder and Wickham disagree on whether making schools gun-free zones increases or decreases the likelihood of school shootings. What do you think? In your opinion, does the fact that your school is a gun-free zone mean it is safer from school shootings or more prone to them? Use evidence from the texts you have read in your answer.

Arming Students Will Prevent School Shootings

Michelle Malkin

In the following essay Michelle Malkin argues that allow-ing students to carry guns will prevent school shootings. She complains that schools have become places that coddle young people, teaching them to be both intel-lectually and physically submissive. As a result, they are at a loss to defend themselves when a school shooter strikes. Malkin says if students were allowed to carry guns, school shootings would be rarer and would kill fewer people if and when they did occur. In her opinion, instilling a culture of self-defense in America's young people begins with teaching them how to use guns and allowing them to bring weapons to schools to protect themselves.

Malkin is a syndicated columnist and the author of *Unhinged: Exposing Liberals Gone Wild.*

Consider the following questions:

1. What does the term "coddle industries" mean in the context of the essay?
2. In Malkin's opinion, how are the erosion of intellectual self-defense and the erosion of physical defense linked?
3. What two words sum up what Malkin thinks students should be taught to prevent school shootings?

There's no polite way or time to say it: American colleges and universities have become coddle industries. Big Nanny administrators oversee speech codes, segregated dorms, politically correct academic departments and designated "safe spaces" to protect students selectively from hurtful (conservative) opinions—while allowing mob rule for approved leftist positions.

Instead of teaching students to defend their beliefs, American educators shield them from vigorous intellectual debate. Instead of encouraging autonomy, our higher institutions of learning stoke passivity and conflict-avoidance.

And as the erosion of intellectual self-defense goes, so goes the erosion of physical self-defense.

Students Need to Be Taught to Defend Themselves

How do we prevent future school shootings? . . . First, allow teachers to carry guns if they have a concealed carry permit. Secondly, allow any parents to carry and patrol the halls as well. . . . Next we stop teaching our kids that they have no right to protect themselves or others. Evil thrives where no one stands against it, and too many schools teach that self-defense is somehow wrong.

Doug Hagin, "How to Stop School Shootings?" RenewAmerica.us, March 22, 2005. www.renew america.us/columns/hagin/050322.

"What If?"

Yesterday morning [April 17, 2007], as news was breaking about the carnage at Virginia Tech, a reader e-mailed me a news story from last January. State legislators in Virginia had attempted to pass a bill that would have eased handgun restrictions on college campuses. Opposed by outspoken, anti-gun activists and Virginia Tech administrators, that bill failed.

Is it too early to ask: "What if?" What if that bill had passed? What if just one student in one of those classrooms had been in lawful possession of a concealed weapon for the purpose of self-defense?

If it wasn't too early for Keystone Cop [CBS news anchor] Katie Couric to be jumping all over campus security yesterday for what they woulda/coulda/shoulda done in the immediate aftermath of the shooting, and if it isn't too early for *The New York Times* editorial board to be publishing its knee-jerk call for more gun con-

The author disagrees with Virginia Tech associate vice president for university relations Larry Hincker's (pictured) decision to oppose arming students on the school's campus.

trol, it darned well isn't too early for me to raise questions about how the unrepentant anti-gun lobbying of college officials may have put students at risk.

Guns Can Protect Us

The back story: Virginia Tech had punished a student for bringing a handgun to class last spring—despite the fact that the student had a valid concealed handgun permit. The bill would have barred public universities from making "rules or regulations limiting or abridging the ability of a student who possesses a valid concealed handgun permit . . . from lawfully carrying a concealed handgun."

Gun Control Will Not Prevent School Shootings

A 2007 poll found that the majority of Americans think tighter gun control laws cannot effectively stop school shootings— most school shooters will always find a way to get guns.

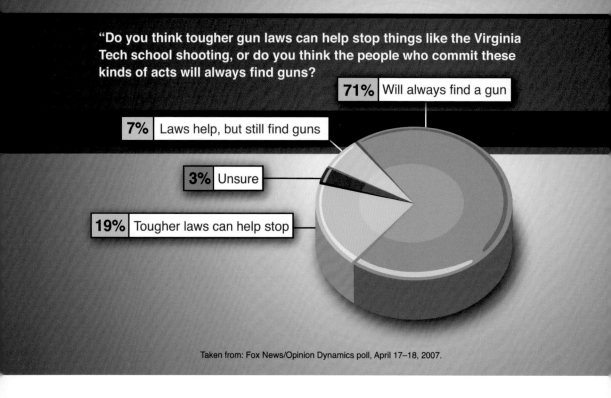

"Do you think tougher gun laws can help stop things like the Virginia Tech school shooting, or do you think the people who commit these kinds of acts will always find guns?

71% Will always find a gun

7% Laws help, but still find guns

3% Unsure

19% Tougher laws can help stop

Taken from: Fox News/Opinion Dynamics poll, April 17–18, 2007.

After the proposal died in subcommittee, the school's governing board reiterated its ban on students or employees carrying guns and prohibiting visitors from bringing them into campus buildings.

Late last summer, a shooting near campus prompted students to clamor again for loosening campus rules against armed self-defense. Virginia Tech officials turned up their noses. In response to student Bradford Wiles's campus newspaper op-ed piece in support of concealed carry on campus, Virginia Tech Associate Vice President Larry Hincker scoffed:

[I]t is absolutely mind-boggling to see the opinions of Bradford Wiles. . . . The editors of this page must have printed this commentary if for no other reason than malicious compliance. Surely, they scratched their heads saying, "I can't believe he really wants to say that." Wiles tells us that he didn't feel safe with the hundreds of highly trained officers armed with high powered rifles encircling the building and protecting him. He even implies that he needed his sidearm to protect himself.

The nerve!

Brady Campaign to Prevent Gun Violence supporters rally in Washington, D.C. The author asserts that the organization's supporters rushed to capitalize on the Virginia Tech shootings in order to promote their agenda.

We Need to Renew a Culture of Self-Defense

Hincker continued: "The writer would have us believe that a university campus, with tens of thousands of young people, is safer with everyone packing heat. Imagine the

continual fear of students in that scenario. We've seen that fear here, and we don't want to see it again. . . . Guns don't belong in classrooms. They never will. Virginia Tech has a very sound policy preventing same."

Who's scratching his head now, Mr. Hincker?

Some high-handed commentators insist it's premature or unseemly to examine the impact of school rules discouraging students from carrying arms on campus. Pundit Andrew Sullivan complained that it was "creepy" to highlight reader e-mails calling attention to Virginia Tech's restrictions on student self-defense—even as the Brady Campaign to Prevent Gun Violence rushed to capitalize on the massacre to sign up new members and gather e-mail addresses for Million Mom March chapters. "We are outraged by the increase in gun violence in America, especially the recent shooting at Virginia Tech," reads the online petition. "Add your name to the growing list of people who are saying: 'Enough Is Enough!'"

Enough is enough, indeed. Enough of intellectual disarmament. Enough of physical disarmament. You want a safer campus? It begins with renewing a culture of self-defense—mind, spirit and body. It begins with two words: Fight back.

Analyze the essay:

1. Malkin quotes several sources in her essay. Make a list of everyone she quotes and what each says. You will notice that everyone she quotes disagrees with her position. Why do you think Malkin chose to quote people who take an opposing view? What does this lend her essay?

2. Malkin blames school shootings in part on a submissiveness that has been cultivated in America's students. What do you think of this charge? Do you agree or disagree? Explain your answer in full.

Arming Students Will Increase School Shootings

Brady Center to Prevent Gun Violence

The Brady Center to Prevent Gun Violence is a nonprofit organization whose goal is to reduce gun violence in America. In the following essay the authors argue that allowing students to carry guns on campus is a dangerous idea and will lead to an increase in school shootings. First, binge drinking and drug use is an increasing problem among student bodies, and the authors say young people cannot be trusted to act responsibly with weapons when they are under the influence so often. Second, young people grapple with mental and emotional issues that threaten their stability—the authors point out that allowing them access to guns during vulnerable or depressed periods poses a serious danger to themselves and others. The center also claims that students are more likely to have their weapons stolen from them and to use weapons accidentally. For all of these reasons, the authors conclude that arming students will increase the number of school shootings, not reduce them.

Consider the following questions:

1. According to the authors, what percent of violence against students occurs off campus? How does this factor into the authors' argument?
2. In what percent of college suicides do the authors say alcohol is a factor? What percent of rapes?
3. How many firearms were reported stolen between 1993 and 2002, according to the authors?

Brady Center to Prevent Gun Violence, *No Gun Left Behind: The Gun Lobby's Campaign to Push Guns into Colleges and Schools.* Washington, DC: Brady Center to Prevent Gun Violence, 2007. Copyright © 2007 Brady Campaign to Prevent Gun Violence. Reproduced by permission.

Despite the horrific massacre at Virginia Tech [on April 16, 2007], college and university campuses are much safer than the communities that surround them. A U.S. Justice Department study found that from 1995 to 2002, college students aged 18 to 24 experienced violence at significantly lower average annual rates—almost 20% lower—than non-students in the same age group. Moreover, 93% of the violence against students occurs off campus. Even 85% of the violent crimes against students who live on campus occur at locations off campus. . . .

Drugs, Alcohol, . . . and Guns?

The prevalence of alcohol and drugs on college campuses is a prime reason to keep guns out. Binge drinking is highest among 18–24-year-olds. Illegal drug use also peaks during these volatile years. Both activities are common among college students. For example, according to a new study by the National Center on Addiction and Substance Abuse at Columbia University, "[n]early half of America's 5.4 million full-time college students abuse drugs or drink alcohol on binges at least once a month." For college gun owners, the rate of binge drinking is even higher—two-thirds. Of course, both drug and alcohol use greatly increases the risks of injury to users and those around them. Alcohol, for example, "is involved in two thirds of college student suicides, in 90% of campus rapes, and in 95% of the violent crime on campus."[1] Almost 700,000 students between the ages of 18 and 24 are assaulted each year by another student who has been drinking. If guns were involved, those assaults would

> ## Arming Students Is a Recipe for Disaster
>
> Safety officers say they would have a more difficult time responding to an active shooter if others are armed in the same area. Armed students could inadvertently add to the mayhem rather than stop violence.
>
> *Midwest Voices*, "Don't Let Students Carry Guns on Missouri's Campuses," April 20, 2009. http://voices.kansascity.com/node/4306.

1. Matthew Miller, David Hemenway & Henry Wechsler, *Guns at College*, 48 J. Am. College Health 7 (1999) (citing Commission on Substance Abuse at Colleges and Universities, *Rethinking Rites of Passage: Substance Abuse on America's Campuses* (1994)).

be much more likely to be fatal. Guns, alcohol, and drugs have proven to be an extremely dangerous mix. Drinking alcohol can even make a police officer "unfit for duty."[2]

There is also a strong connection between gun ownership by college students and an increased likelihood to engage in dangerous activities. Two studies of college students found that those who owned guns were more likely than the average student to:

The Brady Center cites two studies that found students who owned guns were more likely than the average student to get into trouble with the police.

- Engage in binge drinking,
- Need an alcoholic drink first thing in the morning,
- Use cocaine or crack,
- Be arrested for a DUI,
- Vandalize property, and
- Get in trouble with police.

2. Michael Wilson, *Policy for Police Force: Guns and Drunkenness Don't Mix*, New York *Times*, Jan. 30, 2006 (quoting New York Police Department Patrol Guide, which states: "Members of the service SHOULD NOT be in possession of their firearms if there is any possibility that they may become unfit for duty due to the consumption of intoxicants.").

College Gun Owners Are Dangerous

Moreover, the students that engaged in multiple dangerous activities on this list were even more likely to own a gun. Gun ownership was also significantly greater among college students who had either been injured in alcohol-related fights or car accidents than students who were not injured at all. The researchers concluded that *"college gun owners are more likely than those who do not own guns to engage in activities that put themselves and others at risk for severe or life-threatening injuries."* In addition, substance use, school problems, and perpetration of violence have been significantly associated with gun-carrying adolescents.

Colleges and universities have many programs in place to address drug and alcohol abuse, but it is unlikely that campus drug and alcohol problems will be eliminated any time soon. Therefore, it is even more critical that schools be able to ban or tightly control firearms possession and use by students. A binge-drinking, drug-using student is dangerous enough; let's not give him or her a gun.

Students Are Moody and Unstable

Mental health issues and the risks of suicides among college students is another prime reason to prohibit or limit access to guns by college students. Researchers have found that youths aged 18–25 experience the highest rate of mental health problems. According to the American College Health Association's National College Health Assessment, between 9 and 11% of college students seriously considered suicide in the last school year. Even more alarming, every year about 1,100 college students commit suicide and another 24,000 attempt to do so.

Introducing firearms into this psychological cauldron could dramatically increase the danger to students. If a gun is used in a suicide attempt, more than 90% of the time the attempt will be fatal. By comparison, suicide

The United States Leads the World in School Shootings

School shootings occur in other countries, but not as often as in the United States.

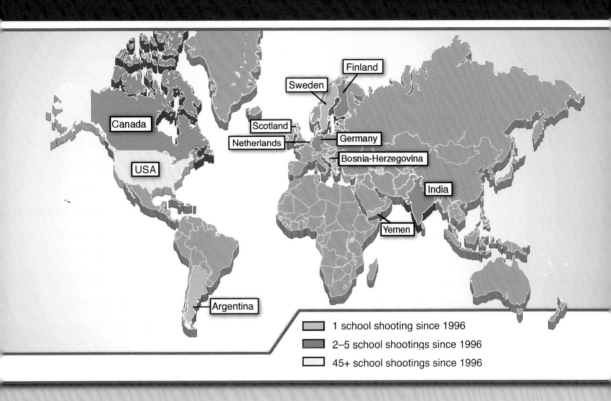

Finland

Sweden

Canada

Scotland

Netherlands

Germany

Bosnia-Herzegovina

USA

India

Yemen

Argentina

☐ 1 school shooting since 1996

▨ 2–5 school shootings since 1996

☐ 45+ school shootings since 1996

Taken from: Mibazaar.com and InfoPlease.com, March 12, 2009.

attempts made by overdosing on drugs are fatal only 3% of the time. Thus, while suicides involving firearms account for only 5% of the suicide attempts in America, they accounted for more than half of the 32,439 fatalities. Needless to say, increasing firearms availability for college students could lead to a significant increase in the number of fatalities among the 24,000 suicide attempts survived by students each year. After all, the

A Cherokee County, Georgia, sheriff shows stolen assault weapons and ammo found at the local high school campus, hidden there by would-be student gunmen.

presence of a gun in the home increases the risk of suicide fivefold.

An Easy Way to Reduce Risks

Colleges and universities have devoted considerable resources to address mental health problems and suicide risks on campus. One thing they have not done, however, is attempt to expel all the students that pose mental health or suicide risks. Nor should they. A college may face legal problems if it discriminates against certain students based on a perception that they are prone to depression or violence. Moreover, many scholars believe it is not possible to reliably identify who will go on a rampage, thus suggesting there is no way for a college or university to distinguish in advance between gun-toters who pose extraordinary risks, and those who may not. According to Dr. James Alan Fox, Dean of the College of Criminal Justice at Northeastern University and one of America's leading criminologists:

> It's not a matter of identifying problem cases and dealing with them. It's a matter of changing the way things are done. . . . You can't just grease the squeaky wheel. You've got to grease the whole machine.

Accordingly, the only safe and non-discriminatory way to reduce the risks of gun violence on college campuses is to keep them gun-free.

The Danger from Stolen or Lost Guns

Increasing gun ownership among college students, especially if they live in campus dorms, is also likely to provide a prime, tempting target for gun thieves. Between 1993 and 2002, nearly 1.7 million firearms were reported stolen to police. The U.S. Justice Department has found that 10% of prison inmates incarcerated on gun charges obtained their gun by stealing it. Stolen guns have already been the source of school shootings in Jonesboro, Arkansas, Springfield, Oregon, and elsewhere.

Most guns that are stolen are taken from homes or parked cars. But these targets seem extremely hardened compared to the ease with which guns could be stolen out of college dorm rooms. Dorm rooms are small, limiting the number of places where guns could be hidden or locked up. They often experience considerable numbers of visitors, some of whom might decide to pinch a firearm if they see one, given their resale value on the illegal market. It is also unlikely that college gun owners will be able to keep secret the fact that they have a gun or guns, and many may openly flaunt this fact. Of course, this will also make it easier for gun thieves to learn where the guns are and steal them.

Once a gun is stolen, it is much more likely to be used in subsequent crime. Thus, if the sensible policies currently in place at nearly all colleges and universities nationwide are replaced by widespread student ownership of firearms, not only will the danger to students on and off campus increase, but so will the danger to surrounding communities.

The best deterrent to firearms theft on college campuses is obviously not to permit students to possess firearms at all. Without guns there can be no gun thefts. Colleges that require students to lock up firearms in a facility managed by campus security or local police also dramatically reduce the risks of gun theft.

Accidental Shootings

In addition to the risk factors above, allowing more guns on college campuses and into schools is likely to increase the risk of students being shot accidentally. Guns in the home are four times as likely to be used in unintentional shootings than in self-defense. Plus, a 1991 report by the General Accounting Office that surveyed unintentional firearm fatalities found that 23% of those deaths occurred because the person firing the gun was unaware whether the gun was loaded. The report explains several ways in which this happens. "For example, one might empty a firearm but not notice that a round remains in the chamber, one might typically leave a weapon unloaded and so assume that it is always unloaded, or one might pull the trigger several times without discharge (dry-firing) and so assume the chamber is empty even though it is not." These mistakes are not limited to children. Even trained gun users have made them.

If there are no guns on campus, these types of accidents cannot occur. . . .

Guns Make People Scared and Unsafe

Rather than making anyone feel safer, allowing students to possess and use firearms on college campuses will likely breed fear and paranoia among fellow students since no one will know whether the other person can simply retrieve or pull out a gun if a dispute arises. Such fear and paranoia is antithetical to creating the kind of climate where free and open academic debate and learning thrive.

In one national study of gun-owners and non-gun-owners alike, 71% of those surveyed said they would feel less safe if more people in their community acquired guns. Among non-gun-owners, the numbers were even higher, with 85% indicating that the increased presence of guns in their neighborhood would lessen their safety. Even among gun owners, roughly half did not want more people to acquire guns. Although this study focused on the increased presence of guns in homes, it offers a powerful message to legislators that may be considering requiring colleges and schools to allow guns. How could it possibly be a good idea to increase fear and anxiety levels among college students?

Moreover, will parents be more or less likely to spend tens of thousands of dollars to send their child to a college or university that permits widespread gun possession and use among its students? No one needs a Ph.D to understand that introducing guns among binge-drinking, drug-using, suicide-contemplating, hormone-raging college students would not help a parent sleep more easily at night. We are not suggesting that these risky behaviors are exhibited by a majority of college students. But they are exhibited frequently enough that it would be unconscionable to introduce guns into these settings. Accordingly, it is not surprising that public surveys have found overwhelming opposition to possession or carrying of guns on college campuses.

Analyze the essay:

1. To make their argument against arming students, the authors describe college students as "binge-drinking," "drug-using," "suicide-contemplating," and "hormone-raging." Do you think this is an accurate description of college students? Does it help convince you that students should not be allowed to carry guns on campus? Why or why not?

2. Several authors in this section make the argument that schools remain one of the safest places for young people. Make a list of each essay that uses this argument, and how they do so. Then, state whether you agree. Do you feel safe at your school? Would you feel more or less safe if guns were allowed on campus? Explain your reasoning.

School Shooters Share a Common Profile

Jessie Klein

In the following essay Jesse Klein argues that school shooters are not deranged individuals but rather share a common profile. She explains that school shooters are often bullied or picked on by their fellow students. Being targeted by others leads them to develop a quiet rage that explodes in a school shooting incident. School shooters are also likely to have been rejected by girls, according to Klein. She explains that the killers involved in the Virginia Tech; West Paducah, Kentucky; Edinboro, Pennsylvania; and Columbine school shootings were all somehow rejected or enraged by members of the opposite sex. Finally, school shooters share a hatred for wealthy, privileged students, in Klein's opinion. She cites examples of school shooters who have targeted rich students in their rampages and discussed their hatred for the upper class in their suicide notes. For all of these reasons, Klein argues that school shootings should not be viewed as isolated incidents by crazed individuals, but rather as a direct response to common problems faced by young people.

Klein is a professor of sociology and criminology at Adelphi University. She has worked in the New York City public schools and has a forthcoming book with Rutgers University Press titled *The Bully Society: School Shootings, Gender, and Other Violence in American Schools.*

Consider the following questions:

1. In how many school shootings over the last decade was bullying a factor, according to Klein?
2. Who did Michael Carneal, Mitchell Johnson, Andrew Golden, and Andrew Wurst target when they shot up their schools?
3. What effect can antibullying programs have on school shootings, in Klein's opinion?

"You have vandalized my heart, raped my soul and torched my conscience," the 23-year-old Virginia Tech gunman, Cho Seung-Hui declared before killing 33 people on campus, including himself. "You thought it was one pathetic boy's life you were extinguishing. Thanks to you, I die like Jesus Christ to inspire generations of the weak and the defenseless people."

We need to listen to Cho's words and heed his concerns as he eerily echoes those of previous school shooters outraged at what they perceived as an unjust school hierarchy that used them as the pariahs to reinforce their own social status and power. Yet in this tragedy, as in past school shootings, authorities ignore the shooters' own explanations for their crimes, instead labeling the horror as merely an aberration. The mental illness that may well have plagued Cho is only a piece of a story. As we mourn the victims of the terror Cho wrought at Virginia Tech, we need also to ask how the bullying he experienced may have pushed him over the edge.

School Shooters Have Usually Been Bullied

Contrary to the views of experts like former Homeland Security Director, Tom Ridge, who said Cho was just "deranged," peers of many of the perpetrators of past similar crimes concede that those young men were bullied relentlessly. "Luke was picked on for as long as I can remember," explained a classmate of sixteen-year-old Luke Woodham, who killed his ex-girlfriend and her best friend and injured seven others in the 1997 school shooting in Pearl, Mississippi. "I do this on behalf of all kids who have been mistreated," Luke also declared.

While their reactions were heinous and reprehensible, these are not random, unprovoked acts of violence but rather a common grievance among many American students. Most react more quietly with suicide, depression, anxiety, truancy, and other more self-destructive responses.

Bullying instigated over 40 school shootings that took place during the past decade. Cho, like the other shooters, had difficulty with girls (stalking two who reported him to the police, speaking often of an "imaginary

The author argues that Virginia Tech shooter Cho Seung-Hui, left, and Paducah, Kentucky, shooter Michael Carneal were not deranged but mad at girls who had rejected them.

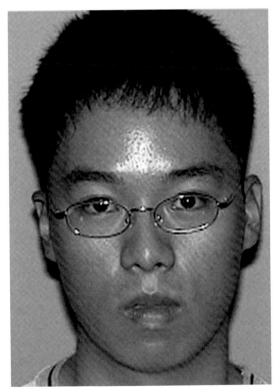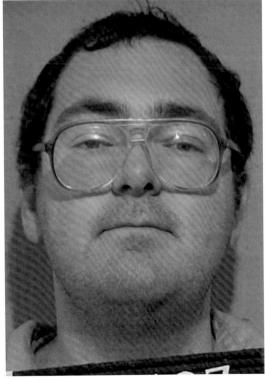

girlfriend," and making many uncomfortable by taking photos of their legs in classes). Like the other perpetrators, he was relentlessly bullied and angry at what he perceived as an unjust school hierarchy that privileges the wealthy. Cho was also bullied as a result of his race: "Go back to China" his peers said to him on one of the rare times he mustered up the courage to speak in class.

This dynamic was also in play at Columbine High School, which until Virginia Tech was the most infamous school shooting. Eric Harris and Dylan Klebold, age 17 and 18, also did not meet the narrow social expectations expected of them at school. They said they were treated like dirt by fellow students and declared their unwillingness to accept the bullying that seemed to have become a socially acceptable and daily form of violence: "Your children who have ridiculed me, who have chosen not to accept me, who have treated me like I am not worth their time are dead. . . ." railed Eric.

School Shooters Have Usually Been Rejected by Girls

In every school shooting, boys targeted girls who rejected them, boys who called them gay or otherwise belittled them, and other students at the top of the school's hierarchy—white, wealthy, and athletic—and then shot down other students in an effort to reinstate their injured masculinity.

In 1997 in West Paducah, Kentucky, 14-year-old Michael Carneal killed three girls, two of whom had rejected him. The following year, in Jonesboro, Arkansas, 13-year-old Mitchell Johnson and 11-year-old Andrew Golden shot their ex-girlfriends as well as two other girls who refused Mitchell's advances. Mitchell "vowed to kill all the girls who broke up with him" and threatened other girls for even speaking about these rejections. His ex-girlfriend complained that Mitchell was stalking her and had even hit her, but no one responded to her concerns. In Edinboro, Pennsylvania, that same year,

14-year-old Andrew Wurst targeted his ex-girlfriend at a school dance. He threatened her prior to the shooting when she first broke up with him. "Then I'll have to kill you," he said. At Columbine, Dylan and Eric were known to have big problems with girls. Dylan was so shy with girls that his parents paid him $250 to attend the Columbine High School Prom.

Boys are taught to believe that sexual interest from a girl is imperative to affirm their manhood. When boys are rejected by girls, it can bring up fears that they are not perceived by others as strong and powerful and can cause many to doubt their masculinity and heterosexuality. Headlines about Cho confirmed he struggled with these same concerns about his manhood.

> ## School Shooters Tend to Share a Set of Characteristics
>
> [Of the] individuals involved in the 7 deadly high school shootings within the past decade, 3 of the shooters had all 10 characteristics, 3 had 8 characteristics, and 1 had 6 characteristics. These characteristics included a desire for attention, rejection from peers, social isolation, angry outbursts, violent threats, a lack of empathy, and a tendency to dehumanize others.
>
> Marlene Busko, "Perpetrators of Deadly School Shootings Seem to Fit 'Cynically Shy' Profile," *Medscape Medical News*, September 4, 2007. www.medscape.com/viewarticle/562375.

A Shared Hatred for the Rich

Cho also raged against the rich, declaring his shooting a response to the "brats" and "snobs" at his school who were not satisfied with their "gold necklaces" and "Mercedes." Cho, whose parents ran a dry cleaner, seemed to believe that the relentless bullying he experienced was a result of his lower economic status and his race.

In high schools as well as colleges, popular kids tend to be wealthier and the boys at the top of school caste are often perceived as "jocks." Those that don't fit into these categories are often teased, or seen as relatively unimportant or even invisible. The boys who killed generally came from less wealthy backgrounds than those they targeted and almost all of them specifically aimed at those perceived as wealthy and popular: the "jocks and preps" in the school who were also the ones who bullied them. Like Luke, Michael, and Eric & Dylan and

What Motivates a School Shooter?

A national Internet survey asked 2,017 public school students in grades 7–12 to rate possible factors that would motivate a school shooter.

Rate	Reasons	Percent Agreeing
1	They want to get back at those who have hurt them.	87
2	Other kids pick on them, make fun of them, or bully them.	86
3	They do not value life.	62
4	They have been victims of physical abuse at home.	61
5	They have mental problems.	56
6	It is easy for them to get a gun.	56
7	They do not get along with their parents.	55
8	They have witnessed physical abuse at home.	54
9	They drink alcohol or use drugs.	52
10	They do not have any good friends.	49
11	They see violence on TV, in movies, and in computer and video games.	37
12	Violence is a way of life in their neighborhood.	34
13	Other kids encouraged them to do it.	28
14	Their teachers do not care about them.	26
15	They are afraid for their own safety.	20
16	They are bored.	18

Taken from: Edward Gaughan, 2001.

many others, sixteen-year old Evan Ramsey, who killed two students and injured two others in Alaska in 1997, had been picked on by popular football players, whom he targeted in his shooting after an argument with one of them.

A Deadly Rite of Passage

Classmates at Columbine High School described how the jocks teased Eric and Dylan. "Everyone would make fun of them" said Ben Oakley from the soccer team. And senior Dustin Thurmon, from the Columbine wrestling team repeated what many others expected: "They should have been able to take it."

But children in our schools should not have to take it. Repeatedly, teachers, parents, and other adults and students say that bullying is a normal part of school life, a rite of passage, or simply a case of "boys will be boys" and sometimes "girls will be girls." Yet my research has traced bullying as a cause of almost every school shooting to date and other research shows that bullying can lead to suicide, severe depression and anxiety, truancy, and dropping-out of school. We need to find a way to stop bullying in schools and to refute assumptions that this behavior is normal.

Many shooters blamed adults for not protecting them from daily assaults. Eric Harris continued: "Teachers, parents, let this massacre be on your shoulders until the day you die." He echoed Evan's words who said after his shooting: "I figured since the principal and the dean weren't doing anything that was making any impression, that I was gonna have to do something, or else I was gonna keep on getting picked on."

School Shooters Are Not Deranged

These shootings are not just aberrations of deranged individuals. They are a reprehensible and unconscionable retaliation to common and real pain felt by students across our nation. Those who solely blame mental illness miss the real concerns about bullying these boys raise, troubles sadly shared by between 25 and 80% of students, according to various studies. We need to examine the persistently cruel school social hierarchies that so many young boys have declared the source of their unbearable misery. Time and again these boys beg for help from adults who either ignore the bullying or impose "zero tolerance" policies—suspending students for any hint of impending violence—that tend to punish minor infractions which often miss the big picture. Our students must feel more supported and accepted by one another independent of race, class, and success with the opposite sex. Stalking was an issue in many of the school shooting cases, as well as sexual harassment, dating violence, and gay-bashing—some of which were issues at Virginia Tech. These concerns must be taken seriously and never written off as "normal bullying."

Now we flip-flop between ignoring bullying altogether, considering it "normal" and implementing "zero tolerance" policies that don't address the relationships among students and between students and adults. We need instead to create communities in schools and raise awareness of all parties involved including victims, bullies, and bystanders so that school hierarchies are dismantled and students treat each other with sincere appreciation and respect. European countries have implemented such community-oriented programs with national policies that already reduced bullying by fifty percent. The Netherlands launched such a program in over 10,000 schools that spread like wildfire through Europe. Here we are still using zero tolerance with zero evidence that any of it is working. We have no national policies and only scattered efforts that try to improve relationships between students and among students and adults. If we don't listen to the terrifying words sung repeatedly by each school shooter, we are sadly likely to see many more such horrors.

Analyze the essay:

1. The author of this essay is a professor of sociology and criminology. She also worked for eleven years in the New York City public schools. Does knowing the author's professional background influence the opinion you have of her argument? If so, in what way? If not, why not?

2. Klein claims that school shooters share a specific set of traumatic experiences. How do you think Joseph Gasper, author of the next essay, would respond to this claim? Use evidence from both texts in your answer.

A School Shooter Has No Specific Profile

Joseph Gasper

In the following viewpoint Joseph Gasper argues there is no specific profile of a school shooter. Contrary to popular opinion, he says, school shooters do not have much in common with each other. Since school shooters are teens, Gasper says they have yet to completely develop emotionally or psychologically, and thus it is difficult to pin down specific characteristics about them since teenage characteristics change so quickly. Furthermore, the characteristics people usually assign to school shooters—being loners, rejected by girls, or bullied, for example—are experiences shared by nearly every single kid in high school. Yet Gasper points out school shootings are very rare, meaning that every kid who has been bullied or rejected is not driven to go on a shooting spree. Gasper concludes that society should stop perpetuating myths about school shooters and realize the factors that drive kids to commit murder are multifaceted and complex.

Gasper is a doctoral student in sociology at the Johns Hopkins University, where he teaches courses on school violence.

Consider the following questions:

1. Why does Gasper think it is unlikely that watching media footage of school shootings will spawn copycat shootings?
2. Why, in Gasper's opinion, is it impossible to identify one single cause of school shootings?
3. What does the term "false positives" mean in the context of the essay?

This week's [2007] shooting incident at Virginia Tech has spawned intense media coverage, much of which has served to perpetuate myths about school shootings.

School Shootings Are Not on the Rise

The first myth is that this latest shooting is a point in an escalation of such incidents. Although rampage school shootings increased during the 1990s, after the terrorist attacks of Sept. 11, 2001, school shootings virtually came to a halt. One explanation is that school officials have gotten better at foiling shooting plots before they materialize. Furthermore, since the 1970s, most types of school crime have declined or remained unchanged.

School is still one of the safest places for young people. In-school homicides and suicides account for only a small percentage of the total number of juvenile homicides and suicides.

The author says it is a myth that media coverage of school shootings inspire copycat killings.

The Myth of Copycat Shootings

The second myth concerns the effect of mass media on copycat shootings. Some have called for a toning down of the coverage of the shooting on the grounds that it may lead to copycat shootings. Sound arguments can be made for squelching the media hype (such as not wanting to create fear of school crime), but a concern over copycat killings is not one of them.

It is unlikely that watching footage of school shootings will increase the likelihood of violent crime. Unlike other forms of media violence (such as violent video games), the violence in the news is not glorified, and the shooter is not portrayed as a hero. Mass media may affect the modus operandi [literally, "mode of operation"] of those already bent on a shooting, but media attention is unlikely to lead otherwise law-abiding young people to commit school shootings. In addition, responsible journalism has the potential to reduce the number of school shootings by making students, teachers, school administrators and others more aware of the causes and warning signs and more likely to report a problem when they see one.

School Shooters Are Not All Alike

The media does the public a major disservice by trying to convince us that there is such a thing as a particular profile that these shooters fit. They try to fit all these ghastly events into a single personality type that we can be afraid of, but it's just not so.

Dave Cullen, "The Myth of the School Shooter Profile," TalkLeft.com, April 18, 2007. www.talkleft.com/story/2007/4/18/13241/8124.

There Is No Single Cause of School Shootings

The third myth is that it is possible (or desirable) to isolate a single cause of school shootings. Many have singled out such explanations as a culture of violence, easy access to guns, violent video games, bullying and the use of prescription drugs, including antidepressants. Although all of these factors can likely be implicated in school shootings, it is usually impossible to identify a single factor that leads someone to commit a school shooting. This is because many students are affected by at least one of

School Shootings in the United States

School shootings have occurred in more than half of all states and killed hundreds of students, teachers, and administrators.

Florida	West Virginia
Lake Worth	Sheperdstown–Sheperd University

Illinois	Minnesota
DelKalb–Northern Illinois University	Red Lake–Red Lake High School Cold Spring–Rocori High School

California	Arizona
Oxnard Santee–Santana High School San Diego–San Diego State University Los Angeles–University of California, Los Angeles	Tucson–University of Arizona Nursing College

Tennessee	Georgia
Memphis (2) Fayetteville	Savannah–Beach High School

	Michigan
	Morris Township–Buell Elementary School Lansing

Louisiana	New Mexico
Baton Rouge–Louisiana Technical College Baton Rouge–Louisiana State University Campbell County–Campbell County High School	Deming

	Oregon
	Springfield

Ohio	Arkansas
Portsmouth–Notre Dame Elementary School	Jonesboro

	Kentucky
	West Paducah–Heath High School

New Jersey	Mississippi
Newark–Mount Vernon School	Pearl

Virginia	Alaska
Blacksburg–Virginia Tech Grundy–Appalachian School of Law	Bethel

	Washington
	Moses Lake

Pennsylvania	Iowa
Lancaster–Amish schoolhouse Red Lion–Red Lion Junior High School Edinboro	Iowa City–University of Iowa

Wisconsin	New York
Cazenovia–Weston School	Brooklyn–New York Technical College Olean

Colorado	Texas
Bailey–Platte Canyon High School Littleton–Columbine High School	Austin–University of Texas, Austin

Compiled by editor.

these factors, and yet the vast majority of students are not school shooters. Rather, attention should be paid to the cluster of factors that leads to school shootings.

It Is Impossible to Profile School Shooters

The fourth myth is that it is possible to construct a criminal profile of a school shooter. Profiling of school shooters is notoriously difficult and unreliable. Because factors implicated in school shootings describe many students, any profile would necessarily produce a large number of "false positives." Fortunately, school shootings are rare events, and there are only a handful of cases on which to construct a valid profile. Also, criminal profiling is designed to predict who will commit crimes, not where they will commit them.

Another impediment to profiling, especially of adolescents, is that they are not fully developed psycho-

The author argues that isolating a single cause for school shootings, such as the influence of violent video games, is not possible because they are caused by a number of factors.

logically or emotionally, and it may be difficult to pin down the psychological and social characteristics of shooters if they change over time. Moreover, profiling may increase feelings of persecution on the part of a potential shooter, increasing the likelihood of an attack. Finally, many legal issues would arise in the use of profiles.

School Shootings Are Not Spontaneous

The fifth myth is that the shooter simply "cracked" or succumbed to a "trigger." In the immediate wake of Virginia Tech shooter Cho Seung-Hui's rampage, some commentators pointed to possible romantic rejection as such a trigger. While school shooters (and mass murderers in general) have often had their masculinity called into question through rejection by girls, being teased for being "gay" or possessing feminine physical characteristics, a school shooting is not a spontaneous act. Rather, the idea tends to enter the shooter's mind long before he pulls the trigger, and many shooters take a great deal of pride in "putting on a show" to prove to others that they are not "wimps." The killing is one last attempt at solving the shooter's social problems.

School Shooters Are Not Always Loners

The final myth involves the importance of mental illness. Although most school shooters have been diagnosed with mental disorders, in many cases, the diagnoses occurred after the shooting. School shooters are often portrayed as unpopular loners who suffer from psychological problems. However, school shooters are not typically without friends—although these friends are often members of unpopular or marginalized social groups.

Mental disorders in place before a shooting may prevent an individual from dealing with stressors—such as social isolation—with which mentally healthy young people would be able to cope, and may reduce inhibitions to violence. However, if we are to prevent school shootings, we need to move past individualistic explanations that rely on mental illness, and move toward a more comprehensive understanding of how society drives such individuals to kill.

Analyze the essay:

1. Jessie Klein, author of the previous essay, would probably disagree with almost every point Joseph Gasper makes. There is one point, however, on which both authors probably agree. Identify this point and explain why they would both agree.

2. In this essay Gasper uses history, examples, and persuasive reasoning to make his argument that there is no profile of a school shooter. He does not, however, use any quotations to support his point. If you were to rewrite this essay and insert quotations, what authorities might you quote from? Where would you place these quotations to bolster the points Gasper makes?

Section Two:
Model Essays
and Writing
Exercises

The Five-Paragraph Essay

An *essay* is a short piece of writing that discusses or analyzes one topic. The five-paragraph essay is a form commonly used in school assignments and tests. Every five-paragraph essay begins with an *introduction*, ends with a *conclusion*, and features three *supporting paragraphs* in the middle.

The Thesis Statement. The introduction includes the essay's thesis statement. The thesis statement presents the argument or point the author is trying to make about the topic. The essays in this book all have different thesis statements because they are making different arguments about school shootings.

The thesis statement should clearly tell the reader what the essay will be about. A focused thesis statement helps determine what will be in the essay; the subsequent paragraphs are spent developing and supporting its argument.

The Introduction. In addition to presenting the thesis statement, a well-written introductory paragraph captures the attention of the reader and explains why the topic being explored is important. It may provide the reader with background information on the subject matter or feature an anecdote that illustrates a point relevant to the topic. It could also present startling information that clarifies the point of the essay or put forth a contradictory position that the essay will refute. Further techniques for writing an introduction are found later in this section.

The Supporting Paragraphs. The introduction is followed by three (or more) supporting paragraphs. These are the main body of the essay. Each paragraph presents and develops a *subtopic* that supports the essay's thesis statement. Each subtopic is spearheaded by a *topic sentence* and supported by its own facts, details, and examples. The writer can use various kinds of supporting material and details to back up the topic of each supporting paragraph. These may include statistics, quotations from people with special knowledge or expertise, historic facts, and anecdotes. A rule of writing is that specific and concrete examples are more convincing than vague, general, or unsupported assertions.

The Conclusion. The conclusion is the paragraph that closes the essay. Its function is to summarize or reiterate the main idea of the essay. It may recall an idea from the introduction or briefly examine the larger implications of the thesis. Because the conclusion is also the last chance a writer has to make an impression on the reader, it is important that it not simply repeat what has been presented elsewhere in the essay but close it in a clear, final, and memorable way.

Although the order of the essay's component paragraphs is important, they do not have to be written in the order presented here. Some writers like to decide on a thesis and write the introduction paragraph first. Other writers like to focus first on the body of the essay and write the introduction and conclusion later.

Pitfalls to Avoid

When writing essays about controversial issues such as school shootings, it is important to remember that disputes over the material are common precisely because there are many different perspectives. Remember to state your arguments in careful and measured terms. Evaluate your topic fairly—avoid overstating negative qualities of one perspective or understating positive qualities of another. Use examples, facts, and details to support any assertions you make.

The Cause-and-Effect Essay

The previous section of this book provided samples of published persuasive writing on school shootings. All are persuasive, or opinion, essays making certain arguments about school shootings. They are also either *cause-and-effect* essays or used cause-and-effect reasoning. This section will focus on writing your own cause-and-effect essay.

Cause and effect is a common method of organizing and explaining ideas and events. Simply put, cause and effect is a relationship between two things in which one thing makes something else happen. The *cause* is the reason why something happens. The *effect* is what happens as a result.

A simple example would be a car not starting because it is out of gas. The lack of gas is the cause; the failure to start is the effect. Another example of cause-and-effect reasoning is found in Viewpoint Two. Author Larry Elder describes how gun-free zones cause school shootings by helping shooters feel unchallenged—they know that no one else on school grounds will be carrying a gun.

Not all cause-and-effect relationships are as clear-cut as these two examples. It can be difficult to determine the cause of an effect, especially when talking about society-wide causes and effects. For example, smoking and cancer have been long associated with each other, but not all cancer patients smoke, and not all smokers get cancer. It took decades of debate and research before the U.S. surgeon general concluded in 1964 that smoking cigarettes causes cancer (and even then, that conclusion was disputed by tobacco companies for many years thereafter). Similarly, in Viewpoint One, author DeWayne Wickham argues that gun-free zones are *not* the cause of school shootings. He argues that easy access to weapons is the primary cause of school shootings; therefore Americans' access to guns should be controlled. As this example shows, creating and evaluating cause and effect involves both collecting convincing evidence and exercising critical thinking.

Types of Cause-and-Effect Essays

In general, there are three types of cause-and-effect essays. In one type, many causes can contribute to a single effect. Supporting paragraphs would each examine one specific cause. For example, in Viewpoint Five Jessie Klein argues that several factors create a school shooter. Bullying, a rejection by girls, and a hatred for the rich are the causes; together they have motivated dozens of school shooters to kill their classmates and teachers—the effect.

Another type of cause-and-effect essay examines multiple effects from a single cause. The thesis posits that one event or circumstance has multiple results. An example from this volume is found in Viewpoint Four by the Brady Center to Prevent Gun Violence. The Brady Center argues that a single cause—arming students— can have multiple effects on school campuses, including increasing suicide rates, increasing accidental shootings, and increasing fear and anxiety levels among students. Arming students is the single cause; increased violence and anxiety are the multiple effects.

A final type of cause-and-effect essay is one that examines a series of causes and effects—a "chain of events"—in which each link is both the effect of what happened before and the cause of what happens next. Model Essay Three on page 74 of this book provides one example. The author describes the story of Steven Kazmierczak, who killed five people at Northern Illinois University on February 14, 2008. A fascination with horror movies, Hitler, and the Bible caused Kazmierczak to develop antisocial ideas and behaviors. In high school, problems with girls compounded his social awkwardness; he attempted suicide and spent the next few years very depressed and heavily medicated. These are just a few events in a chain that led him to commit the "Valentine's

Day Massacre" and an example of a chain-of-events sequence in which an initial cause can have successive repercussions down the line.

Tips to Remember

In writing argumentative essays about controversial issues such as school shootings, it is important to remember that disputes over cause-and-effect relationships are part of the controversy. School shootings and their related issues are complex matters that have multiple effects and multiple causes, and often there is disagreement over what causes what. One needs to be careful and measured in how arguments are expressed. Avoid overstating cause-and-effect relationships if they are unwarranted.

Another pitfall to avoid in writing cause-and-effect essays is to mistake chronology for causation. Just because event X came before event Y does not necessarily mean that X caused Y. Additional evidence may be needed, such as documented studies or similar testimony from many people. Likewise, correlation does not necessarily imply causation. Just because two events happened at the same time does not necessarily mean they are causally related. Again, additional evidence is needed to verify the cause-effect argument.

In this section, you will read some model essays on school shootings that use cause-and-effect arguments and do exercises that will help you write your own.

Words and Phrases Common in Cause-and-Effect Essays

accordingly	it then follows that
as a result of	since
because	so
consequently	so that
due to	subsequently
for	therefore
for this reason	this is how
if . . . then	thus

Video Games Do Not Cause School Shootings

Editor's Notes The first model essay argues that video games do not encourage students to go on shooting sprees. The author offers three reasons that video games have no bearing on a student's decision to shoot others. The essay is structured as a five-paragraph essay in which each paragraph contributes a supporting piece of evidence to develop the argument.

The notes in the margin point out key features of the essay and will help you understand how the essay is organized. Also note that all sources are cited using Modern Language Association (MLA) style.* For more information on how to cite your sources see Appendix C. In addition, consider the following:

1. How does the introduction engage the reader's attention?
2. What cause-and-effect techniques are used in the essay?
3. What purpose do the essay's quotes serve?
4. Does the essay convince you of its point?

■ Refers to thesis and topic sentences

■ Refers to supporting details

Paragraph 1

After every horrific school shooting, there is the inevitable chorus of voices that cry out for Americans to blame video games for the violent, hideous actions of a troubled young person. But the connection between video games and school shootings has always been very weak, and emerging evidence shows there is probably no relationship between games and a person's decision to shoot his or her classmates and teachers.

This is the essay's thesis statement. It tells what main point the essay will argue.

* Editor's Note: In applying MLA style guidelines in this book, the following simplifications have been made: Parenthetical text citations are confined to direct quotations only; electronic source documentation in the Works Cited list omits date of access, page ranges, and some detailed facts of publication.

Paragraph 2

One reason that video games do not contribute to school shootings is that the fantasy world of a video game has very little to do with the reality of a school shooting. Kids know the difference between fantasy and reality; just because they enjoy chasing monsters or killing villains on a TV screen does not mean they are acting out a desire to do so in real life. Furthermore, video games do not teach the skills needed to conduct a mass shooting. Karen Sternheimer, a sociologist at the University of Southern California and author of the book *Kids These Days: Facts and Fictions About Today's Youth*, points out that video games did not teach Virginia Tech shooter Seung-Hui Cho any skills required to shoot thirty-two people on April 16, 2007. Many of the victims were shot at point-blank range, and Cho himself did not play video games. Moreover, journalist Winda Benedetti says most shooting games like "Counter-Strike" primarily promote communication and teamwork. "It can be hard [for non-gamers to] fathom how players who love to run around gunning down their virtual enemies do not have even the slightest desire to shoot a person in real life," she says (Benedetti).

Paragraph 3

Another reason that video games are unlikely to contribute to school shootings is because video game sales do not correspond to school shooting incidents. In fact, youth violence rates on the whole have declined in the years since video game sales have skyrocketed. This was the outcome of a 2008 study by Christopher J. Ferguson, a Texas A&M professor who found that video game sales—which have peaked in the twenty-first century— correspond to some of the lowest youth violence rates seen in more than a decade. In 1996, for example, about 15 million units of video games were sold; serious violent crimes committed by youth, however, were at a ten-year high of more than 170. Eight years later, in 2004, however, youth violence plummeted to just over 60 seriously violent incidences, while video game sales peaked at more than 50 million units sold. Ferguson says such data make it clear that video game sales are not to blame for youth violence like school shootings. "This would be akin to lung cancer *decreasing radically* after smoking cigarettes was introduced into a population, which is simply not the case" (Ferguson 33).

These statistics help support the paragraph's main idea: that video game sales do not correspond to school shooting incidents. Get in the habit of supporting the points you make with facts, quotes, statistics, and anecdotes.

Paragraph 4

Finally, video games are unlikely to have anything to do with school or other types of shootings simply because of the sheer number of people who play them. According to the Entertainment Consumers Association, more than 30 million Americans play video games—surely, if video games were training and encouraging people to go on shooting rampages, then we would see millions of shooters taking up arms, not just the random gunman here and there. The American public agrees that video games are wrongly singled out when it comes to assigning blame for school shootings. In fact, a CBS poll taken about the 1999 Columbine shootings found that while 40 percent blamed the shootings on a lack of parental attention to children, just 8 percent blamed exposure to violent media such as video games.

What is the topic sentence of Paragraph 4? Look for a sentence that tells generally what the paragraph's main point is.

"If . . . then" statements keep the ideas in a cause-and-effect essay moving. See Preface B for a list of words and phrases commonly found in cause-and-effect essays.

Paragraph 5

It is more likely that America's school shootings are caused by a complicated blend of factors, such as a psychologically troubled person having easy access to a gun. Bullying and a deepening disregard for humanity brought on by the Iraq War are also probably more to blame than video games. As Ferguson urges, "We must move past the moral panic on video games and other media and take a hard look at the real causes of serious aggression and violence" (33–34). After all, video games are a relatively recent phenomenon; murder, on the other hand, is not.

Note how the essay's conclusion wraps up the topic in a final memorable way—without repeating the points made in the essay.

Works Cited

Benedetti, Winda. "Were Video Games to Blame for Massacre? Pundits Rushed to Judge Industry, Gamers in the Wake of Shooting." MSNBC.com 20 Apr. 2007 < http://www.msnbc.msn.com/id/18220228// > .

Ferguson, Christopher J. "School Shooting/Violent Video Game Link: Causal Relationship or Moral Panic?" *Journal of Investigative Psychology and Offender Profiling* 2008: 25–37. Syndicat National du Jeu Video. < http://www.snjv.org/data/document/school-and-violence.pdf > .

Exercise 1A: Create an Outline from an Existing Essay

It often helps to create an outline of the five-paragraph essay before you write it. The outline can help you organize the information, arguments, and evidence you have gathered during your research.

For this exercise, create an outline that could have been used to write "Video Games Do Not Cause School Shootings." This "reverse engineering" exercise is meant to help familiarize you with how outlines can help classify and arrange information.

To do this you will need to

1. articulate the essay's thesis,
2. pinpoint important pieces of evidence,
3. flag quotes that supported the essay's ideas, and
4. identify key points that supported the argument.

Part of the outline has already been started to give you an idea of the assignment.

Outline
I. Paragraph One
Write the essay's thesis:

II. Paragraph Two
Topic: Just because kids kill things in video games does not mean they are acting out a desire to do so in real life.

   Supporting Detail i.

   Supporting Detail ii. Quote from Winda Benedetti about how video games foster communication and team work, not a desire to kill.

III. Paragraph Three
Topic: Video game sales do not correspond to school shooting incidents.

i.

ii. Quote from Christopher Ferguson about how linking video games with school shootings makes as much sense as linking a decline in cancer to the advent of smoking.

IV. Paragraph Four
Topic:

i. There are more than 30 million Americans who play video games, and the overwhelming majority of these people do not become shooters.

ii.

V. Paragraph Five
i. Write the essay's conclusion:

Teachers Should Not Be Allowed to Carry Guns at School

Editor's Notes The second model essay embodies a more specific form of the cause-and-effect essay: It describes multiple effects from a single cause. In the case of this essay, the author argues that arming teachers with guns would have multiple negative effects on a school. Arming teachers is the cause; making guns more accessible to students, making it more likely innocents are killed, and scaring the student body are the effects. In clear, distinct paragraphs the author outlines these different effects and supports her points with facts, anecdotes, and quotes.

As you did for the first model essay, take note of the essay's components and how they are organized (the sidebars in the margins will help you identify the essay's pieces and their purpose).

■ Refers to thesis and topic sentences

■ Refers to supporting details

Paragraph 1

Everyone is upset when news breaks about a school shooting—the tragic and needless loss of life is a blow and a threat to every American. Yet some have suggested responding to the problem by allowing teachers to carry guns on school property. This is a terrible idea, as arming teachers would have at least three negative effects on schools and student bodies.

This is the essay's thesis statement. It tells what main points the essay will argue.

Paragraph 2

Allowing teachers to keep guns in their classrooms puts the guns at risk of being stolen by students. After all, answer keys, tests, and high-end equipment are stolen from classrooms by students every day. Do we want to add guns to the list of items that could be taken from a teacher's desk or cabinet? Students who are aware of their teacher's ability to keep a gun in the classroom would likely try to steal it or might even wrestle it away

What is the topic sentence of Paragraph 2? Look for a sentence that tells generally what the paragraph's main point is.

from him or her during a crisis. Supporters of arming teachers argue guns could be kept away from students in a secure safe—but locking them up defeats the purpose of having them in the classroom at all. As the Brady Center argues, "Aside from the exorbitant cost, [a safe] makes it even less likely the gun could be used to stop a school shooting, given the time it would take to retrieve the weapon" (Brady Center 11). Furthermore, teachers who are known to carry a gun are probably going to be the first people targeted by the school shooter.

What point in Paragraph 2 does this quote directly support?

Paragraph 3

Secondly, if teachers are allowed to carry arms at school, more people are likely to get shot and die in the event of a school shooting. Teachers are trained to be teachers, not security guards or police officers. According to the Brady Center, even trained police officers hit their intended targets less than 20 percent of the time. It stands to reason that teachers—even ones who have experience with firearms and target practice regularly—would not be as good a shot as a police officer. Counting on teachers to fire on school shooters, therefore, is likely to create a lot of crossfire that will probably kill innocent people.

Make a list of all the transitions that appear in the essay and how they keep the ideas moving.

Paragraph 4

Finally, putting an armed teacher in front of a class threatens the psychological health of the entire student body. Many students have never seen a gun—surely their teacher, the person who is entrusted with their day-to-day education and development, should not be the first person to brandish one in front of them. Students are likely to be intimidated by gun-toting teachers, afraid to speak their mind or even go to them for extra help. Indeed, arming teachers creates an environment that is antithetical to learning. If anyone is to carry a gun at school, let it be a more appropriate figure, such as a security guard. A statewide poll conducted in 2008 by the *Mobile Press-Register*/University of South Alabama found that the majority of Alabamans—who are typically very

What is the topic sentence of Paragraph 4? How did you recognize it?

pro-gun—think that if guns are to be found on school campuses, only security guards should be authorized to carry them. Fifty-two percent said they disapproved of professors and teachers being armed in the classroom; 41 percent favored it, while 11 percent were unsure. If a pro-gun state like Alabama is hesitant to let teachers carry guns, it should tell us something about the inappropriateness of the idea.

This fact supports one of the paragraph's main ideas: that teachers should not be armed. Support the points you make with facts, quotes, and statistics.

Paragraph 5

Arming teachers will turn schools into prisons and teachers into guards. Guns have no place in an institution of higher learning, or at least in the possession of those charged with educating our young people. Let us look for solutions to school shootings not by introducing more guns into the school environment but by making sure it is harder for would-be school shooters to get their hands on one in the first place.

Look at Exercise 3A on conclusions. What type of conclusion is this? Does it close the essay in a final and memorable way?

Works Cited

"No Gun Left Behind: The Gun Lobby's Campaign to Push Guns into Colleges and Schools." Brady Center to Prevent Gun Violence May 2007 < http://www.bradycenter.org/ xshare/pdf/reports/no-gun-left-behind.pdf > .

Exercise 2A: Create an Outline from an Existing Essay

As you did for the first model essay in this section, create an outline that could have been used to write "Teachers Should Not Be Allowed to Carry Guns at School." Be sure to identify the essay's thesis statement, its supporting ideas, its descriptive passages, and key pieces of evidence that were used.

Exercise 2B: Create an Outline for Your Own Essay

The second model essay expresses a particular point of view about school shootings. For this exercise, your assignment is to find supporting ideas, choose specific and concrete details, create an outline, and ultimately write a five-paragraph essay making a different, or even opposing, point about school shootings. Your goal is to use cause-and-effect techniques to convince your reader.

Step One: Write a thesis statement.
The following thesis statement would be appropriate for a multiple-effects essay on why teachers should be allowed to carry guns at school:

> **Teachers can be the first line of defense against school shooters—if armed, they can take down the shooter infinitely faster than the police or an armed guard stationed elsewhere on school grounds.**

Or see the sample paper topics suggested in Appendix D for more ideas.

Step Two: Brainstorm pieces of supporting evidence.
Using information from some of the viewpoints in the previous section and from the information found in Section Three of this book, write down three arguments or pieces of evidence that support the thesis statement you selected. Then, for each of these three arguments, write down supportive facts, examples, and details that support it. These could be:

- statistical information;
- personal memories and anecdotes;
- quotes from experts, peers, or family members;
- observations of people's actions and behaviors;
- specific and concrete details;
- convincing and logical cause-and-effect reasoning.

Supporting pieces of evidence for the above sample topic sentence are found in this book, and include:

- Statistic in Appendix A about how a 2008 poll taken by *Education Week* found that 83 percent of those polled believed teachers should be allowed to carry guns at school.
- Story told in Viewpoint Two by Larry Elder about assistant principal Joel Myrick, who kept a school shooter subdued with his .45 automatic until police arrived on campus. Myrick ran to his truck to get his gun; Elder argues that had he been allowed to keep it on his person, he could have prevented the deaths of two students.
- Quote from Michelle Malkin in Viewpoint Three: "Enough of intellectual disarmament. Enough of physical disarmament. You want a safer campus? It begins with renewing a culture of self-defense—mind spirit, and body. It begins with two words: Fight back."

Step Three: Place the information from Step Two in outline form.

Step Four: Write the arguments or supporting statements in paragraph form.
By now you have three arguments that support the paragraph's thesis statement, as well as supporting material. Use the outline to write out your three supporting arguments in paragraph form. Make sure each paragraph has a topic sentence that states the paragraph's thesis clearly and broadly. Then, add supporting sentences that express the facts, quotes, details, and examples that support the paragraph's argument. The paragraph may also have a concluding or summary sentence.

Caring Student or Violent Monster? Deconstructing a School Shooter

Editor's Notes The following essay illustrates the third type of cause-and-effect essay: a "chain of events" essay. In this kind of essay, each link in the chain is both the effect of what happened before and the cause of what happens next. In other words, instead of factors A, B, and C causing phenomenon X, the "chain of events" essay describes how A causes B, which then causes C, which in turn results in X. Specifically, the author examines the chain of events that led Steven Kazmierczak to kill five people and himself at Northern Illinois University. Chronology—expressing what events come before and which after—plays an important part in this type of essay.

This essay also differs from the previous model essays in that it is longer than five paragraphs. Sometimes five paragraphs are simply not enough to adequately develop an idea. Extending the length of an essay can allow the reader to explore a topic in more depth or present multiple pieces of evidence that together provide a complete picture of a topic. Longer essays can also help readers discover the complexity of a subject by examining a topic beyond its superficial exterior. Moreover, the ability to write a longer research or position paper is a valuable skill you will need as you advance academically through high school, college, and beyond.

Paragraph 1

On February 14, 2008, Steven Kazmierczak killed five classmates and wounded eighteen others at Northern Illinois University before turning the gun on himself. Though he is most famous for this horrible act, Kazmierczak was also known to the people in his life as being an excellent student and a caring, generous friend. Americans have wondered what could have caused an intelligent, respected person to commit such a ghastly, violent crime. A chain reaction of disturbing events over the course of Kazmierczak's life reveals that this shooting rampage was years in the making, the final battle in a long war with mental illness.

How can you tell this is going to be a cause-and-effect essay?

Paragraph 2

When he was young, Kazmierczak displayed a fascination with violence and death. He enjoyed throwing his pet dog, a pug with breathing problems, against a wall, and also liked to shoot at moving cars with a pellet gun. His interest in mischief and anarchy landed him in police custody as early as the eighth grade, when he and a friend were arrested for exploding a homemade bomb on the porch of a neighborhood house. While in police custody, he named two friends who helped him make the Drano bomb, and as a result became isolated from his social group at school.

How does Paragraph 2 serve to foreshadow what kind of person Kazmierczak would become?

Paragraph 3

Despite being a social outcast at school, Kazmierczak managed to land himself a girlfriend. But she, too, quickly rejected him. Violent outbursts and moodiness at home led his parents to start him on medication for bipolar disorder, but Kazmierczak's mental stability slid downward. In 1996 and 1997 he made three attempts to kill himself—the first by overdosing on Tylenol; the second by overdosing on Ambien and slitting his wrists; the third by overdosing on a drug called Depakote. During this time he was in and out of Alexian Brothers hospital in Elk Grove Village, Illinois, for suicidal thoughts and violent mood swings. Despite the treatment, he made another failed suicide attempt on February 11, 1998.

Paragraph 4

Despite his struggles with suicide, Kazmierczak managed to graduate high school with a "B" average. Instead of going to college like many of his classmates, however, he went to a group home called the Mary Hill Residence, where he was treated for mental illness and obsessive/compulsive disorder (OCD), an anxiety condition in which a person feels compelled to perform irrational, repetitive tasks such as tapping their hands or counting. Yet instead of getting better, his symptoms got worse. He told his therapists he could read minds and had visions of people who were not actually there. He was put on even more medication—over the course of his life he took Clozaril, Cylert, Depakote, lithium, Paxil, Prozac, Risperdal, Seroquel, Xanax, and Zyprexa, an astonishing list of antidepressants and antianxiety medications. But the drugs only made Kazmierczak feel that being medicated was interfering with his ability to get on with his life. He therefore stopped taking his meds, and as a result was asked to leave the group home.

These specific details help you picture what kind of person Kazmierczak was. Always use specific rather than vague details when writing.

Paragraph 5

Seeking a big life change, Kazmierczak next enlisted in the Army on September 5, 2001. He lied on his application, saying he had never attempted suicide or been evaluated or treated for mental illness. The Army suited him—the strict routine and constant orders were a good match for his OCD because his mind had no freedom to wander and worry. He also liked learning how to use professional weapons and did so with an eerie aptitude that signaled the detached brutality with which he would later end his life: "They train him how to shoot, how to kill," describes one reporter who chronicled Kazmierczak's life. "No emotional or psychological response, that's what they're looking for, and he can do this" (Vann).

"Next" is a transitional phrase that lets you know a cause-and-effect relationship is being discussed. What other transitional words and phrases common to cause-and-effect essays are found in this essay?

Paragraph 6

But Kazmierczak was kicked out of the Army in just a few months, after it was discovered he had lied on his application. Desperate to get his life headed in some direction, he enrolled in Northern Illinois University in 2002, where he showed an aptitude for sociology and criminology. The next five years were good for Kazmierczak: He excelled

How is the topic of Paragraph 6 different, but related, to the other topics discussed thus far?

in school, made friends, and had several girlfriends and a serious relationship with a girl named Jessica Baty. He founded the NIU chapter of the American Correctional Association and became its treasurer and vice president. He tutored sociology students and was considered an effective, helpful teacher. He was so highly regarded in school that a professor, Charles Cappell, wrote the following about him in a recommendation letter for graduate school: "[Steve] is extremely patient and calm when tutoring students. . . . He has the highest ethical and academic standards, he thinks abstractly and analytically, and relates at an emotional and empathetic level with others" (qtd. in Vann). He did so well in school he was given a Dean's Award, the highest honor given to undergraduate students at NIU. Given his undergraduate successes, he enrolled in graduate school.

Make a list of everyone quoted in this essay. What types of people have been quoted? What makes them qualified to speak on this topic?

Paragraph 7

Yet underneath these achievements, remnants of the old, disturbed Steve Kazmierczak were lurking and growing stronger. His mother's death in 2006 triggered a downward emotional spiral. He talked obsessively to people about mass murderers like Adolf Hitler and Ted Bundy. He started failing his classes and picked fights with Jessica. They broke up, and he made himself feel better by buying guns. He started spending all his time at shooting ranges and amassing a collection of guns and ammunition. Most tellingly, he showed a fascination with school shootings: When thirty-two people were killed at Virginia Tech on April 16, 2007, Kazmierczak was almost invigorated by the news. He admired the gunman's writings and shooting strategy and became obsessed with learning his favorite songs and where he bought his guns.

What cause-and-effect chain of events is described in Paragraph 7?

Paragraph 8

During the summer of 2007, Kazmierczak recognized that his OCD was coming back and was worse than ever. "He checks five times to make sure the car is locked, three times for the apartment door, checks the stove. He . . . drive[s] somewhere, but he has to turn around, drive back to check again that the door is locked. He washes his hands twenty times a day, has to wash the remote for the TV if anyone else touches it" (Vann). He sought help at a health center on the campus of the University of Illinois where he was taking graduate classes, and for the first time in more than six years was put back on antidepressants.

Paragraph 9

What words and phrases have indicated this is a cause-and-effect essay?

Even though Kazmierczak sought help on his own, he did not stick with it—he went on and off his meds, which made him unstable and unpredictable. He started having random sexual encounters with women he met on the Internet, yet these left him feeling more alone and unfulfilled. He rekindled his obsession with guns and ammunition, and in early 2008 he started amassing a weapons collection. He also started playing a video game that is based on the Virginia Tech shootings and another game called "Call of Duty 4," a first-person shooter game. In an e-mail to a friend, he implied he was practicing with virtual weapons for some unknown purpose.

Paragraph 10

Around February 10, 2008, Kazmierczak set in motion the events that would culminate in his death and the deaths of five others just a few days later. He told friends he was going on a trip to visit his godfather, but instead he booked a hotel room near the NIU campus. For three days he stayed in the hotel room, calling friends and family members to have one last conversation. On the night before February 14, 2008, he deleted all of his e-mails and closed the accounts. He hid the SIM card of his cell phone and the hard drive of his computer, and neither were ever found. He sent a package to his ex-girlfriend Jessica that contained a wedding ring and other gifts, such as an iPhone, earrings, a purse, and CDs.

Paragraph 11

At 3:04 P.M. on Valentine's Day, Kazmierczak burst into a lecture room in Cole Hall on the NIU campus armed with a shotgun and several pistols. The class was an introductory class on ocean science. He walked onto the stage in the front of the hall and began shooting into the crowd. After he wounded eighteen people and killed five, he turned the gun on himself. No one knew why he chose to return to his alma mater to deliver such random violence. Social worker J. Ray Rice guesses that Kazmierczak's accomplishments and reputation at NIU may have been a factor: "Steven was a smart student who may have wanted someone to outsmart him, to identify and rescue him from the pain he was suffering. This may be the reason he chose to return to NIU and kill as many people as possible. He chose to commit suicide on a stage at the university that knew him for being smart."

> Note how the author returns to ideas introduced in Paragraph 1. See Exercise 3A for more on introductions and conclusions.

Paragraph 12

Even after the massacre, friends of Kazmierczak had trouble reconciling the smart, good student with the gunman who had taken the lives of innocent people. Said Alexandra Chapman, "He was one of the most genuine people I have ever met. I want people to know that he was a really great person, that he was just a really great guy, he was so kind and would always do anything for you. So it doesn't make sense. I just don't want people to think of him as a monster" (qtd. in "Gunman, Ex-Honor Student Treated for Mental Illness"). The twists and turns of Kazmierczak's life offer little help in making sense of his violent act. Was he a good, kindhearted friend or a monster? Was he a severely disturbed individual or an accomplished student? Was he a loving boyfriend or a violent, twisted, psychopath? The events of Kazmierczak's life appear to reveal he was all of these people wrapped into one.

> Note the chronological events the author has recounted to get the reader to the point in the story at which Kazmierczak becomes a shooter.

Works Cited

"Gunman, Ex–Honor Student Treated for Mental Illness." ABC Channel 7, Chicago News 15 Feb. 2008 < http:// abclocal.go.com/wls/story?section = news/local&id = 5959663 > .

Rice, J. Ray. "The Hidden Abandonment Issues of a Mass Murder." *It's All About Abandonment* 18 Feb. 2008 < https://www.itsallaboutabandonment.com/Steven_ Kazmierczak-NIU.html > .

Vann, David. "Portrait of the School Shooter as a Young Man." *Esquire* August 2008: 114–27 < http://www.esquire.com/ features/steven-kazmierczak-0808 > .

Exercise 3A: Examining Introductions and Conclusions

Every essay features introductory and concluding paragraphs that are used to frame the main ideas being presented. Along with presenting the essay's thesis statement, well-written introductions should grab the attention of the reader and make clear why the topic being explored is important. The conclusion reiterates the essay's thesis and is also the last chance for the writer to make an impression on the reader. Strong introductions and conclusions can greatly enhance an essay's effect on an audience.

The Introduction

There are several techniques that can be used to craft an introductory paragraph. An essay can start with

- an anecdote: a brief story that illustrates a point relevant to the topic;
- startling information: facts or statistics that elucidate the point of the essay;
- setting up and knocking down a position: a position or claim believed by proponents of one side of a controversy, followed by statements that challenge that claim;
- historical perspective: an example of the way things used to be that leads into a discussion of how or why things work differently now;
- summary information: general introductory information about the topic that feeds into the essay's thesis statement.

1. Reread the introductory paragraphs of the model essays and of the viewpoints in Section One. Identify which of the techniques described above are used in the example essays. How do they grab the attention of the reader? Are their thesis statements clearly presented?

2. Write an introduction for the essay you have outlined and partially written in Exercise 2B using one of the techniques described above.

The Conclusion

The conclusion brings the essay to a close by summarizing or returning to its main ideas. Good conclusions, however, go beyond simply repeating these ideas. Strong conclusions explore a topic's broader implications and reiterate why it is important to consider. They may frame the essay by returning to an anecdote featured in the opening paragraph. Or they may close with a quotation or refer to an event in the essay. In opinionated essays, the conclusion can reiterate which side the essay is taking or ask the reader to reconsider a previously held position on the subject.

3. Reread the concluding paragraphs of the model essays and of the viewpoints in Section One. Which were most effective in driving their arguments home to the reader? What sorts of techniques did they use to do this? Did they appeal emotionally to the reader, or bookend an idea or event referenced elsewhere in the essay?

4. Write a conclusion for the essay you have outlined and partially written in Exercise 2B using one of the techniques described above.

Exercise 3B: Using Quotations to Enliven Your Essay

No essay is complete without quotations. Get in the habit of using quotes to support at least some of the ideas in your essays. Quotes do not need to appear in every paragraph, but often enough so that the essay contains voices aside from your own. When you write, use quotations to accomplish the following:

- Provide expert advice that you are not necessarily in the position to know about.
- Cite lively or passionate passages.
- Include a particularly well-written point that gets to the heart of the matter.
- Supply statistics or facts that have been derived from someone's research.
- Deliver anecdotes that illustrate the point you are trying to make.
- Express first-person testimony.

Problem One:

Reread the essays presented in all sections of this book and find at least one example of each of the above quotation types.

There are a couple of important things to remember when using quotations.

- Note your sources' qualifications and biases. This way your reader can identify the person you have quoted and can put their words in a context.
- Put any quoted material within proper quotation marks. Failing to attribute quotes to their authors constitutes plagiarism, which is when an author takes someone else's words or ideas and presents them as his or her own. Plagiarism is a very serious infraction and must be avoided at all costs.

Write Your Own Cause-and-Effect Five-Paragraph Essay

Using the information from this book, write your own five-paragraph cause-and-effect essay that deals with school shootings. You can use the resources in this book for information about issues relating to school shootings and how to structure a cause-and-effect essay.

The following steps are suggestions on how to get started.

Step One: Choose your topic.

The first step is to decide what topic to write your cause-and-effect essay on. Is there any aspect about school shootings or guns and violence in general that particularly fascinates you? Is there an issue you strongly support or feel strongly against? Is there a topic you feel personally connected to? Ask yourself such questions before selecting your essay topic. Refer to Appendix D: Sample Essay Topics if you need help selecting a topic.

Step Two: Write down questions and answers about the topic.

Before you begin writing, you will need to think carefully about what ideas your essay will contain. This is a process known as *brainstorming*. Brainstorming involves asking yourself questions and coming up with ideas to discuss in your essay. Possible questions that will help you with the brainstorming process include:

- Why is this topic important?
- Why should people be interested in this topic?
- How can I make this essay interesting to the reader?
- What question am I going to address in this paragraph or essay?
- What facts, ideas, or quotes can I use to support the answer to my question?

Questions especially for cause-and-effect essays include:

- What are the causes of the topic being examined?
- What are the effects of the topic being examined?

- Are there single or multiple causes?
- Are there single or multiple effects?
- Is a chain reaction of events involved?

Step Three: Gather facts, ideas, and anecdotes related to your topic.
This book contains several places to find information, including the viewpoints and the appendixes. In addition, you may want to research the books, articles, and Web sites listed in Section Three, or do additional research in your local library. You can also conduct interviews if you know someone who has a compelling story that would fit well in your essay.

Step Four: Develop a workable thesis statement.
Use what you have written down in steps two and three to help you articulate the main point or argument you want to make in your essay. It should be expressed in a clear sentence and make an arguable or supportable point.

Example:
> **The Framers of the Constitution never intended school shootings to result from the "right to keep and bear arms."**
>> This could be the thesis statement of a cause-and-effect essay that argues that gun ownership leads to unnecessary murder and violence, such as school shootings, and as a result should be illegal.

Step Five: Write an outline or diagram.
1. Write the thesis statement at the top of the outline.
2. Write Roman numerals I, II, and III on the left side of the page with A, B, and C under each numeral.
3. Next to each Roman numeral, write down the best ideas you came up with in step three. These should all directly relate to and support the thesis statement.
4. Next to each letter write down information that supports that particular idea.

Step Six: Write the three supporting paragraphs.

Use your outline to write the three supporting paragraphs. Write down the main idea of each paragraph in sentence form. Do the same thing for the supporting points of information. Each sentence should support the paragraph of the topic. Be sure you have relevant and interesting details, facts, and quotes. Use transitions when you move from idea to idea to keep the text fluid and smooth. Sometimes, although not always, paragraphs can include a concluding or summary sentence that restates the paragraph's argument.

Step Seven: Write the introduction and conclusion.

See Exercise 3A for information on writing introductions and conclusions.

Step Eight: Read and rewrite.

As you read, check your essay for the following:

- ✔ Does the essay maintain a consistent tone?
- ✔ Do all paragraphs reinforce your general thesis?
- ✔ Do all paragraphs flow from one to the other? Do you need to add transition words or phrases?
- ✔ Have you quoted from reliable, authoritative, and interesting sources?
- ✔ Is there a sense of progression throughout the essay?
- ✔ Does the essay get bogged down in too much detail or irrelevant material?
- ✔ Does your introduction grab the reader's attention?
- ✔ Does your conclusion reflect on any previously discussed material or give the essay a sense of closure?
- ✔ Are there any spelling or grammatical errors?

Tips on Writing Effective Cause-and-Effect Essays

- You do not need to include every detail on your subjects. Focus on the most important ones that support your thesis statement.
- Vary your sentence structure; avoid repeating yourself.
- Maintain a professional, objective tone of voice. Avoid sounding uncertain or insulting.
- Anticipate what the reader's counter arguments may be and answer them.
- Use sources that state facts and evidence.
- Avoid assumptions or generalizations without evidence.
- Aim for clear, fluid, well-written sentences that together make up an essay that is informative, interesting, and memorable.

Section Three:
Supporting
Research
Material

Facts About School Shootings

Editor's Note: These facts can be used in reports or papers to reinforce or add credibility when making important points or claims.

School Shootings in America

According to SchoolShooting.org, there have been 324 school shootings since 1992; these have resulted in the deaths of more than 175 teachers, students, and shooters.

The top 3 deadliest American shootings to date are:

- April 16, 2007, Virginia Tech, Blacksburg, VA—32 people killed
- April 20, 1999, Columbine High School, Littleton, CO—13 people killed
- December 1, 1997, Heath High School, West Paducah, KY—3 people killed

According to National School Safety and Security Services, there were 272 school-associated violent deaths between 1999 and 2009; 122 of these were shootings:

- 12 were in the 2008–2009 school year
- 16 were in the 2007–2008 school year
- 32 were in the 2006–2007 school year
- 27 were in the 2005–2006 school year
- 39 were in the 2004–2005 school year
- 49 were in the 2003–2004 school year
- 16 were in the 2002–2003 school year
- 17 were in the 2001–2002 school year
- 31 were in the 2000–2001 school year
- 33 were in the 1999–2000 school year

The American Medical Association reports that between 36 percent and 50 percent of male eleventh graders said they could easily get a gun if they wanted one.

According to a report by the Josephson Institute of Ethics, 60 percent of high school and 31 percent of middle school boys said they could get a gun if they wanted to.

According to KnowGangs.com:

- Most school shooters have an above-average IQ;
- few have been formally diagnosed with a mental illness prior to their attacks;
- few have histories of drug or alcohol abuse;
- 75 percent had threatened or tried to take their own life at some point prior to the attack;
- 50 percent of school shooters had been diagnosed with depression prior to the attack;
- 81 percent of all school shooters carried out the attack alone;
- 11 percent carried out the attack alone, but had the assistance of others;
- 8 percent of the time the attack was committed with the immediate assistance of another person;
- half of all school shooters had an interest in video games or movies with a violent theme;
- 66 percent of school shooters interviewed after the attack felt they had been bullied or threatened by classmates and said that was their main reason for shooting others;
- in nearly three out of four school shootings, the shooter had recently experienced a negative change in a significant relationship, such as a romantic rejection;
- in 75 percent of all school shootings, at least one adult had been concerned about the shooter's recent conversations or behavior prior to the shooting;

- in 50 percent of the shootings, at least one adult communicated their concern about the student's behavior prior to the shooting.

According to the Centers for Disease Control and Prevention:

- In 2006 the chance of a student being killed in a school shooting was less than one in a million.
- A child under the age of fourteen is twenty times more likely to drown than to die in a school shooting.

School Shootings Around the World

Europeans have experienced fewer school shootings than Americans, but they do occur there. The following school shootings have been among Europe's deadliest:

- March 11, 2009: seventeen-year-old Tim Kretschmer kills 9 students, 3 teachers, and 3 others before killing himself at a school in Winnendon, Germany. It is Europe's deadliest school shooting to date.
- September 23, 2008: twenty-two-year-old Matti Saari kills 9 fellow students and a teacher before shooting himself at a school in Kauhajoki, Finland.
- November 7, 2007: eighteen-year-old Pekka-Eric Auvinen shoots and kills 8 people and himself at a high school in Tuusula, Finland.
- November 20, 2006: eighteen-year-old Sebastian Bosse goes on a shooting spree at his former high school in Emsdetten, Germany, injuring 4 students and the school janitor. Bosse then kills himself.
- April 26, 2002: nineteen-year-old Robert Steinhaeuser kills 13 teachers, 2 former classmates, and a policeman after being expelled from a school in Erfurt, Germany. He then commits suicide.
- March 13, 1996: forty-three-year-old Thomas Hamilton kills 16 nursery school children and their teacher in Dunblane, Scotland, then shoots himself.

Since 1992, Canada has experienced five school shootings with a cumulative death toll of seven.

School shootings have also taken place in Argentina, Australia, India, Israel, Lebanon, Thailand, the Philippines, and Yemen.

American Opinions About School Shootings

A 2007 Fox News poll found that

- 19 percent of Americans believe tougher gun laws can help stop school shootings;
- 71 percent of Americans believe tougher gun laws cannot help prevent school shootings;
- 7 percent think tougher gun laws can help prevent school shootings, but shooters will probably still find a way to get guns;
- 3 percent are unsure.

A CBS News/*New York Times* poll found that

- 32 percent of Americans think stricter gun laws would have done a lot to prevent the Virginia Tech shootings;
- 21 percent of Americans think stricter gun laws would have done little to prevent the Virginia Tech shootings;
- 43 percent think stricter gun laws would not have prevented the Virginia Tech shootings;
- 1 percent said it would depend;
- 3 percent were unsure;
- 25 percent said allowing adults to carry concealed handguns would have reduced some of the violence at Virginia Tech;
- 45 percent said allowing adults to carry concealed handguns would have had no effect on the violence at Virginia Tech;
- 3 percent said it depends;
- 4 percent were unsure.

According to a 2007 ABC News poll,

- 40 percent of Americans blame pop culture for youth gun violence in America;

- 35 percent of Americans blame poor parenting for youth gun violence in America;
- 18 percent of Americans blame the availability of guns for youth gun violence in America;
- 5 percent and 2 percent, respectively, blame other causes or are unsure.

A 2008 poll conducted by the Virginia Commonwealth University found that

- 69 percent of Virginians think parents need to tell schools about a child's social or emotional problems;
- 18 percent said those details should be kept private.

A CBS News poll taken one year after the Columbine shootings found that parents blamed the event on the following:

- 40 percent said the shooters' parents did not pay adequate attention to them.
- 8 percent said it was the result of TV violence.
- 7 percent blamed the availability of guns.
- 7 percent said the school failed to pay attention to the shooters.
- 6 percent blamed the shooters' psychological problems.
- 5 percent blamed a lack of religion or moral values.
- 5 percent said the shootings resulted from a feeling of frustration.
- 3 percent said a lack of discipline caused the shootings.
- 2 percent said peer pressure contributed to the shootings.
- 7 percent said there was some other cause.
- 10 percent were unsure what caused the shootings.
- 72 percent predicted there would be more school shootings in the future.
- 22 percent believed future school shootings were unlikely to occur.

- 6 percent were unsure.
- 56 percent said school shootings like Columbine can be prevented.
- 37 said school shootings cannot be prevented.
- 7 percent did not know.

A 2008 poll taken by *Education Week* found that 83 percent of those polled believed teachers should be allowed to carry guns to school.

Finding and Using Sources of Information

No matter what type of essay you are writing, it is necessary to find information to support your point of view. You can use sources such as books, magazine articles, newspaper articles, and online articles.

Using Books and Articles

You can find books and articles in a library by using the library's computer or cataloging system. If you are not sure how to use these resources, ask a librarian to help you. You can also use a computer to find many magazine articles and other articles written specifically for the Internet.

You are likely to find a lot more information than you can possibly use in your essay, so your first task is to narrow it down to what is likely to be most usable. Look at book and article titles. Look at book chapter titles, and examine the book's index to see if it contains information on the specific topic you want to write about. (For example, if you want to write about school shootings in Europe and you find a book about gun violence, check the chapter titles and index to be sure it contains information about European school shootings before you bother to check out the book.)

For a five-paragraph essay, you do not need a great deal of supporting information, so quickly try to narrow down your materials to a few good books and magazine or Internet articles. You do not need dozens. You might even find that one or two good books or articles contain all the information you need.

You probably do not have time to read an entire book, so find the chapters or sections that relate to your topic, and skim these. When you find useful information, copy it onto a note card or notebook. You should look for supporting facts, statistics, quotations, and examples.

Using the Internet

When you select your supporting information, it is important that you evaluate its source. This is especially important with information you find on the Internet. Because nearly anyone can put information on the Internet, there is as much bad information as good information. Before using Internet information—or any information—try to determine if the source seems to be reliable. Is the author or Internet site sponsored by a legitimate organization? Is it from a government source? Does the author have any special knowledge or training relating to the topic you are looking up? Does the article give any indication of where its information comes from?

Using Your Supporting Information

When you use supporting information from a book, article, interview, or other source, there are three important things to remember:

1. *Make it clear whether you are using a direct quotation or a paraphrase.* If you copy information directly from your source, you are quoting it. You must put quotation marks around the information and tell where the information comes from. If you put the information in your own words, you are paraphrasing it.

   Here is an example of a using a quotation:

   Emerging research shows that video games do not have any influence on school shooters. Christopher Ferguson, who has studied the video game–school shooting link extensively, says: "The link has not merely been unproven; I argue that the wealth of available data simply weighs against any causal relationship" (34).

Here is an example of a brief paraphrase of the same passage:

> Emerging research shows that video games do not have any influence on school shooters. The results of a 2008 study on the video game–school shooting link found that not only is the relationship untested but that all available data show that video games do not cause school shooters to act.

2. *Use the information fairly.* Be careful to use supporting information in the way the author intended it. For example, it is unfair to quote an author as saying, "Arming teachers and students will help reduce the number of school shootings," when he or she actually said, "How could anyone think that arming teachers and students will help reduce the number of school shootings?" This is called taking information out of context. This is using supporting evidence unfairly.

3. *Give credit where credit is due.* Giving credit is known as citing. You must use citations when you use someone else's information, but not every piece of supporting information needs a citation.

   - If the supporting information is general knowledge—that is, it can be found in many sources—you do not have to cite your source.
   - If you directly quote a source, you must cite it.
   - If you paraphrase information from a specific source, you must cite it.

If you do not use citations where you should, you are *plagiarizing*—or stealing—someone else's work.

Citing Your Sources

There are a number of ways to cite your sources. Your teacher will probably want you to do it in one of three ways:

- Informal: As in the example in number 1 above, tell where you got the information as you present it in the text of your essay.
- Informal list: At the end of your essay, place an unnumbered list of all the sources you used. This tells the reader where, in general, your information came from.
- Formal: Use numbered footnotes or endnotes. Footnotes or endnotes are generally placed at the end of an article or essay, although they may be placed elsewhere depending on your teacher's requirements.

Works Cited

Ferguson, Christopher J. "School Shooting/Violent Video Game Link: Causal Relationship or Moral Panic?" *Journal of Investigative Psychology and Offender Profiling* 2008: 25–37 < http://www.snjv.org/data/document/school-and-violence.pdf > .

Using MLA Style to Create a Works Cited List

You will probably need to create a list of works cited for your paper. These include materials that you quoted from, relied heavily on, or consulted to write your paper. There are several different ways to structure these references. The following examples are based on Modern Language Association (MLA) style, one of the major citation styles used by writers.

Book Entries

For most book entries you will need the author's name, the book's title, where it was published, what company published it, and the year it was published. This information is usually found on the inside of the book. Variations on book entries include the following:

A book by a single author:
> Axworthy, Michael. *A History of Iran: Empire of the Mind.* New York: Basic Books, 2008.

Two or more books by the same author:
> Pollan, Michael. *In Defense of Food: An Eater's Manifesto.* New York: Penguin, 2009.
> ———. *The Omnivore's Dilemma.* New York: Penguin, 2006.

A book by two or more authors:
> Ronald, Pamela C., and R.W. Adamchak. *Tomorrow's Table: Organic Farming, Genetics, and the Future of Food.* New York: Oxford University Press, 2008.

A book with an editor:
> Friedman, Lauri S., ed. *Introducing Issues with Opposing Viewpoints: War.* Detroit: Greenhaven, 2010.

Periodical and Newspaper Entries

Entries for sources found in periodicals and newspapers are cited a bit differently from books. For one, these sources usually have a title and a publication name. They also may have specific dates and page numbers. Unlike book entries, you do not need to list where newspapers or periodicals are published or what company publishes them.

An article from a periodical:
> Hannum, William H., Gerald E. Marsh and George S. Stanford. "Smarter Use of Nuclear Waste." *Scientific American* Dec. 2005: 84–91.

An unsigned article from a periodical:
> "Chinese Disease? The Rapid Spread of Syphilis in China." *Global Agenda* 14 Jan. 2007.

An article from a newspaper:
> Weiss, Rick. "Can Food from Cloned Animals Be Called Organic?" *Washington Post* 29 Jan. 2008: A06.

Internet Sources

To document a source you found online, try to provide as much information on it as possible, including the author's name, the title of the document, date of publication or of last revision, the URL, and your date of access.

A Web source:
> De Seno, Tommy. *"Roe vs. Wade* and the Rights of the Father." The Fox Forum.com 22 Jan. 2009. May 20, 2009 < http://foxforum.blogs.foxnews.com/2009/ 01/22/deseno_roe_wade/ > .

Your teacher will tell you exactly how information should be cited in your essay. Generally, the very least information needed is the original author's name and the name of the article or other publication.

Be sure you know exactly what information your teacher requires before you start looking for your supporting information so that you know what information to include with your notes.

Sample Essay Topics

Topics for Cause-and-Effect Essays

Bullying Causes School Shootings

Bullying Does Not Cause School Shootings

Violent Video Games Cause School Shootings

Violent Video Games Do Not Cause School Shootings

Access to Guns Causes School Shootings

Access to Guns Can Prevent School Shootings

A Lack of Morality Causes School Shootings

The Immaturity of Adolescents Causes School Shootings

Schools Can Prevent School Shootings

Schools Cannot Prevent School Shootings

Access to Mental Health Treatment Can Prevent School
    Shootings

Arming Teachers Can Prevent School Shootings

Arming Teachers Will Cause More School Shootings

Arming Students Can Prevent School Shootings

Arming Students Will Cause More School Shootings

Outfitting Schools with Metal Detectors Can Prevent
    School Shootings

Hiring Armed Guards Will Prevent School Shootings

Hiring Armed Guards Will Not Prevent School Shootings

Topics for Persuasive and Expository Essays

Students Should Be Allowed to Bring Guns to School

Students Should Not Be Allowed to Bring Guns to School

Gun Control Is Needed to End School Shootings

Gun Control Is Not the Answer to School Shootings

The Legality of Guns Is to Blame for School Shootings

Organizations to Contact

The editors have compiled the following list of organizations concerned with the issues debated in this book. The descriptions are derived from materials provided by the organizations. All have publications or information available for interested readers. The list was compiled on the date of publication of the present volume; the information provided here may change. Be aware that many organizations take several weeks or longer to respond to queries, so allow as much time as possible.

The Brady Center to Prevent Handgun Violence
1225 Eye St. NW, Ste. 1100, Washington, DC 20005
(202) 289-7319 • fax: (202) 408-1851
Web sites: www.cphv.org • www.gunlawsuits.org

The center is the legal action, research, and education affiliate of Handgun Control, Inc. The center's Legal Action Project provides free legal representation for victims in lawsuits against reckless gun manufacturers, dealers, and owners. It publishes many reports specific to the problem of school shootings.

Canadians Concerned About Violence in Entertainment (C-CAVE)
167 Glen Rd., Toronto, ON M4W 2W8 Canada
(416) 961-0853 • fax: (416) 929-2720
e-mail: info@c-cave.com • Web site: www.c-cave.com

C-CAVE conducts research on the harmful effects violence in the media has on society and provides its findings to the Canadian government and public. The organization's committees research issues of violence against women and children, sports violence, pornography, and whether media violence influences the actions of school shooters.

Center for the Prevention of School Violence
4112 Pleasant Valley Rd., Ste. 214, Raleigh, NC 27612
(800) 299-6054 • Web site: www.ncdjjdp.org/cpsv/

The Center for the Prevention of School Violence is a primary point of contact for information, programs, and research about school violence and its prevention. As a clearinghouse, it provides information about all aspects of the problems that fall under the heading of school violence, including school shootings.

Coalition to Stop Gun Violence
1424 L St. NW, Ste. 2-1, Washington, DC 20005
(202) 408-0061 • e-mail:csgv@csgv.org
Web site: www.csgv.org

The coalition lobbies at the local, state, and federal levels to ban the sale of handguns and assault weapons to individuals and to institute licensing and registration of all firearms. It also litigates cases against firearms makers and works to raise awareness about how the prevalence of guns in society contributes to school shootings.

Gun Owners of America (GOA)
8001 Forbes Pl., Ste. 102, Springfield, VA 22151
(703) 321-8585 • e-mail: goamail@gunowners.org
Web site: www.gunowners.org

This lobbying organization supports the ownership of guns as an issue of personal freedom and is dedicated to protecting and defending the Second Amendment rights of gun owners. Its online resources include the newsletter *Gunowners*, gun control fact sheets, information about firearms legislation in Congress, and articles that support the arming of students and teachers in an effort to take down school shooters.

Million Mom March
1225 Eye St. NW, Ste. 1100, Washington, DC 20005
(888) 989-MOMS • Web site: www.millionmommarch.org

The foundation is a grassroots organization that supports commonsense gun laws. The foundation organized the Million Mom March, in which thousands marched through Washington, D.C., on Mother's Day, May 14, 2000, in support of licensing and registration and other firearms regulations.

National Alliance for Safe Schools (NASS)

PO Box 335, Slanesville, WV 25444-0335
(304) 496-8100 • e-mail: nass@frontiernet.net
Web site: www.safeschools.org

Founded in 1977 by a group of school security directors, the National Alliance for Safe Schools was established to provide training, security assessments, and technical assistance to school districts interested in reducing school-based crime and violence. It publishes the book *Making Schools Safe for Students*.

National Institute of Justice (NIJ)
National Criminal Justice Reference
Service (NCJRS)

PO Box 6000, Rockville, MD 20849-6000 • (800) 851-3420
e-mail: askncjrs@ncjrs.org • Web site: www.ncjrs.org

A component of the Office of Justice Programs of the U.S. Department of Justice, the NIJ supports research on crime, criminal behavior, and crime prevention. The National Criminal Justice Reference Service acts as a clearinghouse for criminal justice information for researchers and other interested individuals. Among the numerous reports it publishes and distributes are *Addressing Bullying in Schools: Theory and Practice*, *Crime in the Schools: Reducing Conflict with Student Problem Solving*, and *Preventing School Shootings: A Summary of a U.S. Secret Service School Initiative Report*.

National Rifle Association of America (NRA)

11250 Waples Mill Rd., Fairfax, VA 22030
(703) 267-1000 • Web site: www.nra.org

With nearly 3 million members, the NRA is America's largest organization of gun owners. The NRA believes that gun control laws violate the U.S. Constitution and do not reduce crime.

National School Safety Center (NSSC)

141 Duesenberg Dr., Ste. 11, Westlake Village, CA 91362
(805) 373-9977 • fax: (805) 373-9277
e-mail: info@nssc1.org • Web site: www.nssc1.org

The NSSC is a research organization that studies school crime and violence, including school shootings. The center's mandate is to focus national attention on cooperative solutions to problems that disrupt the educational process. NSSC provides training, technical assistance, legal and legislative aid, and publications and films toward this cause.

Office of Juvenile Justice and Delinquency Prevention (OJJDP)

810 Seventh St. NW, Washington, DC 20531
(202) 307-5911 • e-mail: askjj@ojp.usdoj.gov
Web site: http://ojjdp.ncjrs.org

As the primary federal agency charged with monitoring and improving the juvenile justice system, the OJJDP develops and funds programs on juvenile justice. Among its goals are the prevention of school shootings and other serious violent offenses on school grounds.

Second Amendment Foundation

12500 NE Tenth Pl., Bellevue, WA 98005
(425) 454-7012 • Web site: www.saf.org

The foundation is dedicated to informing Americans about their Second Amendment right to keep and bear firearms. The foundation publishes numerous books and articles, many of which are about school shootings.

Second Amendment Research Center
The John Glenn Institute

350 Page Hall, 1810 College Rd., Columbus, OH 43210

(614) 247-6371 • e-mail: 2nd-amend@osu.edu
Web site: www.secondamendmentcenter.org

Based at the John Glenn Institute for Public Service and Public Policy at Ohio State University, the center's goals are to examine how gun violence can be reduced while protecting the rights of gun owners. The organization's Web site is an excellent resource that includes a listing of articles on gun violence and school shootings by experts on both sides of the issue.

U.S. Department of Education
Safe and Drug-Free Schools Program
400 Maryland Ave. SW, Washington, DC 20202
(800) USA-LEARN • (202) 260-3954
e-mail: customerservice@inet.ed.gov
Web site: www.ed.gov

The Safe and Drug-Free Schools Program is the U.S. Department of Education's primary vehicle for reducing illegal and violent activities on school grounds through education and prevention activities in America's schools.

Youth Crime Watch of America (YCWA)
9200 S. Dadeland Blvd., Ste. 417, Miami, FL 33156
(305) 670-2409 • e-mail: ycwa@ycwa.org
Web site: www.ycwa.org

Youth Crime Watch of America is a nonprofit organization that assists youth in actively reducing crime and violence in their schools and communities. Its resources include handbooks for adult advisers and youth on starting and operating a Youth Crime Watch program, a *Getting Started* video, a *Mentoring Activities* handbook, and a *Talking with Youth About Prevention* teaching guide.

Bibliography

Books

Christensen, Loren W., *Surviving a School Shooting—a Plan of Action for Parents, Teachers, and Students.* Boulder, CO: Paladin Press, 2008.

Kass, Jeff, *Columbine: A True Crime Story, a Victim, the Killers and the Nation's Search for Answers.* Denver, CO: Ghost Road, 2009.

Kellner, Douglas, *Guys and Guns Amok: Domestic Terrorism and School Shootings from the Oklahoma City Bombing to the Virginia Tech Massacre.* Boulder, CO: Paradigm, 2008.

Langman, Peter, *Why Kids Kill: Inside the Minds of School Shooters.* New York, NY: Palgrave Macmillan, 2009.

Lebrun, Marcel, *Books, Blackboards, and Bullets: School Shootings and Violence in America.* Lanham, MD: Rowman & Littlefield Education, 2008.

Lieberman, Joseph, *The Shooting Game: The Making of School Shooters.* Santa Ana, CA: Seven Locks, 2006.

Periodicals and Internet Sources

Beneditti, Winda, "Were Video Games to Blame for Massacre? Pundits Rushed to Judge Industry, Gamers in the Wake of Shooting," MSNBC.com, April 20, 2007. www.msnbc.msn.com/id/18220228//.

Cullen, Dave, "The Myth of the School Shooter Profile," Talk Left.com, April 18, 2007. www.talkleft.com/story/2007/4/18/13241/8124.

Deacon, Michael, "Don't Blame Germany's School Shooting on a Video Game," *Telegraph* (London), March 14, 2009. www.telegraph.co.uk/comment/4991340/Dont-blame-Germanys-school-shooting-on-a-video-game.html.

Doheny, Kathleen, "What Triggers School Shooters? Cynical Shyness Common in Shooters, Often Linked with

Violence, Researchers Say," CBS News.com, August 20, 2007. www.cbsnews.com/stories/2007/08/20/health/webmd/main3185030.shtml.

Ferguson, Christopher J., "School Shooting/Violent Video Game Link: Causal Relationship or Moral Panic?" *Journal of Investigative Psychology and Offender Profiling*, 2008. www.snjv.org/data/document/school-and-violence.pdf.

Hagin, Doug, "How to Stop School Shootings?" RenewAmerica.us, March 22, 2005. www.renewamerica.us/columns/hagin/050322.

Helmke, Paul, "When a School Shooter Seeks a License to Carry a Loaded, Concealed Handgun," HuffingtonPost.com, December 23, 2008. www.huffingtonpost.com/paul-helmke/when-a-school-shooter-see_b_153194.html.

Kelley, Tina, "In an Era of School Shootings, a New Drill," *New York Times*, March 25, 2008. www.nytimes.com/2008/03/25/nyregion/25drills.html.

Lithwick, Dahlia, "Teen Terror: Are Teenagers Like Fundamentalist Terrorists?" Slate.com, August 12, 2006. www.slate.com/id/2147496/.

Luik, John, "Bulletproofing Canada: Gun Control Won't Prevent School Shootings. But Having Guns Might Help Individuals Mitigate Them," *Western Standard*, May 21, 2007.

Newman, Katherine S., "Finding Causes of Rampage Shootings Is One Thing; Preventing Them Is Another," *Chronicle of Higher Education*, April 19, 2007. http://chronicle.com/cgi2-bin/printable.cgi?article = http://chronicle.com/free/2007/04/2007041904n.htm.

Pancevskiin, Bojan, "Mass Killer 'Rejected' by Girl at Party," *Times* (London), March 15, 2009. www.timesonline.co.uk/tol/news/world/europe/article5908602.ece.

Paterson, Tony, "In Europe's League of School Shootings, Germany Comes Top," *Independent* (London), March 15, 2009.

Reese, Charley, "School Shooters," LewRockwell.com, March 28, 2005. www.lewrockwell.com/reese/reese177.html.

Shapiro, Svi, "Virginia Tech: Education and a Culture of Death," *Tikkun,* July/August, 2007.

Silverman, Daniel, "Student Privacy Versus Campus Security: An Overstated Conflict," *Human Rights,* Summer 2008.

Simon, Stephanie, "Guns Belong in Schools, Dealer Says; Online Seller Whose Products Were Used in 2 High-Profile Shootings Argues More Firearms Will Make Students Safer," *Chicago Tribune,* March 5, 2008.

Toppo, Greg, "10 Years Later, the Real Story Behind Columbine," *USA Today,* April 14, 2009. www.usatoday.com/news/nation/2009-04-13-columbine-myths_N.htm.

Unruh, Bob, "Are Meds to Blame for Cho's Rampage?" *World Net Daily,* April 23, 2007. www.worldnetdaily.com/news/article.asp?ARTICLE_ID = 55310.

Vann, David, "Portrait of the School Shooter as a Young Man," *Esquire,* August 2008.

Welch, William M., "Va. Tech Gunman Sent Material to NBC," *USA Today,* April 18, 2007. www.usatoday.com/news/nation/2007-04-18-virginia-tech_N.htm.

White, Daniel, "Another School Shooting Makes Gun Control the Topic of the Day," *Cleveland Gun Rights Examiner,* March 12, 2009. www.examiner.com/x-2206-Cleveland-Gun-Rights-Examiner ~ y2009m3d12-Another-school-shooting-makes-Gun-control-the-topic-of-the-day.

Web Sites

American School Counselor Association School Shooting Resources Page (www.schoolcounselor.org/content.asp?contentid = 524%20). This page, maintained by the national organization of school counselors, offers articles and tips for how to deal with students during and after a crisis such as a school shooting or the death of a classmate.

Keep Schools Safe (www.keepschoolssafe.org). Keep Schools Safe helps teachers, school administrators, parents, and students prevent violence in schools. The Web site is presented in the style of a blog and contains breaking news on school violence around the world and offers tips for what to do if a shooter enters your school.

Keys to Safer Schools (www.keystosaferschools.com). This site offers educators, parents, and teachers methods and techniques that will help reduce school violence. The Web site has a map of all school shootings that have taken place in the United States.

National School Safety and Security Services (www.schoolsecurity.org). An excellent resource for students looking for statistics on school shootings and other forms of school violence.

SchoolShooting.org (http://schoolshooting.org). This Web site was launched on April 20, 2009, the ten-year anniversary of the Columbine High School shooting. It seeks to establish the most comprehensive database of school shooting incidents in the United States. It is maintained by the National School Safety Center.

Index

Picture Credits

About the Editor

Lauri S. Friedman earned her bachelor's degree in religion and political science from Vassar College in Poughkeepsie, New York. Her studies there focused on political Islam. Friedman has worked as a non-fiction writer, a newspaper journalist, and an editor for more than ten years. She has extensive experience in both academic and professional settings.

Friedman is the founder of LSF Editorial, a writing and editing business in San Diego. She has edited and authored numerous publications for Greenhaven Press on controversial social issues such as oil, the Internet, the Middle East, democracy, pandemics, and obesity. Every book in the *Writing the Critical Essay* series has been under her direction or editorship, and she has personally written more than eighteen titles in the series. She was instrumental in the creation of the series, and played a critical role in its conception and development.